WILLIAM MACKENZIE

A New Beginning

Written by

Mackenzie William Moulton

Outline of the opening to a new Crime Novel, written by Mackenzie William Moulton (ex police diver and dive supervisor)

William Mackenzie is the main character in the story.

He was a policeman for 20 years, serving for 10 years as a police diver in the Metropolitan Police.
Mac, as his friends know him, is a member of the elite Underwater Search and Security Unit (USU).

The Unit are on a routine search of City Airport Docks when an underwater pre-planted bomb explodes, killing three officers in the team.

Mac, who should have been in the water is, saved by a fluke fault with his breathing apparatus.

He was close enough to the blast for his hands to be badly burnt.

An official investigation into the explosion is started and as time goes on all is not quite as straightforward as it should be.

Mac is unable to prove that anything was wrong with his equipment compounded by a rumour that he himself had missed the explosives.

The pressure slowly begins to build on Mac.
His damaged hands leave him house bound and left alone to think.

On the worst day of his life he discovers not only has his wife been involved in a long-term affair, but also the bomb was in the section he gave the all clear to.

The shock, pressure and frustrations of the current situations send him over the edge.

Mac is admitted to Hospital, thrown out of the force and the enquiry is nicely closed much to the delight of his senior officers.

Mac decides he has to start anew, to see more of the UK, and get away from the horrible events that have ruined his career and marriage.

A motor caravan seems to be the perfect answer and he buys the biggest and best on the market, after all this will be his only home for sometime to come.

Mac heads South West towards his roots.

Away from London and seeing life in a new light, the events of the last five months are not what they first seemed.

Now for his own sanity and peace of mind he still wants to know the truth.

Mac turns back towards London.
For him the enquiry is not finished and a new beginning starts.

Our Two Main Characters:

Our main story concerns William Mackenzie.
Forbes, his brother, is an integral part of the plot.

Both are serving members of the London Metropolitan Police Force; Mac, with the Underwater Search Unit, and Forbes as a detective. They are not based at the same station.

The brothers have a good degree of intelligence and integrity.
Mac is more of a manly, fit, rugged outdoor man.
Forbes is the typical English middle-aged man, slightly overweight and unfit.

POSSIBLE CONTINUING STORIES

After his name is cleared Mac decides against returning to the British Police Force and sticks to his original plan of exploring the UK in his motor caravan.

This leaves endless possibilities in Mac's further adventures and the travels of William Mackenzie (Mac)

With his motor caravan, he is free to travel anywhere-Wales, Scotland, or Europe.

He becomes the unsuspecting Private Investigator with added diving skills.
He is the reluctant knight in shining armour.

Mac would rather stay single, yet romance seems to come his way adding to his dilemmas.

His brother, who is still in the police force, can be a constant reference point for information needed in Mac's investigations.

Having only one main character – Mac - each story is in a new location and brings a new set of people making it of interest to everyone around the UK.

Mac understands what it's like to lose, and to have to struggle to regain one's life.
In the stories, we are aware of his constant energy and incandescence.

There will be a gritty realism and strength to Mac's stories.
Unintentionally he has become the roaming detective who cannot help but get involved in local mysteries and unsolved crimes.

Chapter 1

Explosion

Present time.

A large motor caravan has just joined the M4 motorway heading away from London. On the back is a scrambler motorbike.
Inside the motor caravan, it is panelled in dark wood, but the atmosphere is light and airy with several framed drawings on the walls.

The pictures have no overriding theme, yet there is an anger and passion about them. There's a half finished drawing of a Dalmatian dog on the side. On the floor is a diver's aqualung mask and fins.
Driving the motor caravan is a half-shaven man, 42ish, named William Mackenzie, Mac to his friends.
As Mac drives along the long boring motorway, his mind drifts back to some months before.

Flash-back

Inside a Portacabin located on the edge of the dock area now known as London City Airport, Mac sits drinking a cup of tea. The Portacabin is being used as a briefing area and it's full of policemen, some dressed in combat uniform with trousers tucked into their boots, and four others dressed in red divers' dry suits. Mac is wearing a diver's dry suit and so is Bruce Frazer. Bruce is a man of 33. He is very fit, handsome and distinctive looking, with short blond hair.

Sergeant Tony Hayes, 42 years old, and an unapproachable type, is standing by a large map of the Docks and airport. In his hand is a sheet of paper, the heading reads, Underwater Search Unit Dive Roster.
Tony looks at the dive roster and says, 'John and Chris, you are in section A and B. Mac and Bob section C and D. Bruce and Lee in E and F.'
Someone breaks wind, loudly, a few laughs are heard. Tony keeps a straight face saying, 'What's this, a farm-yard?'

Chris, 34, is a tall thin but very fit man, is wearing a dive suit made to measure because he is so tall. It fits him like a glove.
He puts his hand in the air and says in a broad Scottish accent, 'There are a few pigs in here, Sarge!' Everyone laughs.
Tony laughs too and continues, 'Someone has twice had a go at this Carlos Azeglio, I don't want to have to explain to every Tom Dick and Harry why they got third time lucky here, because there's not going to be a third time. Comprende?'
Smoothy, 35 years old, a short stocky and balding member of the team, pipes up, 'I thought in Italy, they cut something off and stuck it in your mouth?'
John, 34 years old who looks like a rugby player, with a thick black beard to go with his thick London accent, replies, 'I'd rather get blown up mate.'
Everyone laughs except Tony who stares at John. There is a short silence. 'Sorry Sarge.'

Tony waits for a moment looks around the Portacabin and says, 'OK then, thank you gents, you all know what you have to do, we have to get this done today and before six. Smoothy and I will be in section G and K.'

All the necessary equipment for this security operation was put into the dive lorry the night before, as it was going to be an early start at the Airport. The diving vehicle, a 14 ton box lorry, was specially designed to be a self-contained unit for the divers should they be away from other facilities for a long time. It has seating for eight personnel, cooking facilities, washing and toilet facilities and the ability to carry all sorts of commercial diving equipment and medical equipment.

The diving lorry arrives at a jetty attached to the side of the runway that serves the London City Airport. The whole area is busy with police carrying out their various duties. Police sniffer dogs, trained to sniff out explosives, are seen checking out anything that may hide a bomb. Surface search teams probe boxes, bins, and look down drains for anything that may be suspicious.

As the diving lorry pulls up at the jetty, the team immediately leaps out and into action, each member knowing his job. Search lines are placed into the water; divers are assisted into their dry suits, and

helped with their air tanks and weights and within no time the first diver is in the water.

As Mac and Bruce step onto the jetty, Mac says, 'What happened to you last night?'
Bruce replies, 'I promised to look after my sister's little girl, then sis was late, you know the usual nonsense. Chris tells me I missed a good night?'
With a grin on Mac's face, he says, 'Well Chris was kissing the stripper, that's why he had a good night.'
Sergeant Tony Hayes comes up behind them. 'You're always the last two in the water.'
Mac quickly replies. 'We were debating the pro's and con's of these luxurious waters.'

London City Airport was built on Docklands and is surrounded by water. Most of the water is 8 to 12 metres deep. The bottom is littered with cars, shopping trolleys, barbed wire, bottles and all sorts of unpleasant hazards, not to mention all the nasty bugs one could catch. It's an area of water the dive team has dived many times before, recovering anything from dead bodies to safes, guns and stolen property.

With a smile on his face Tony says, 'Get a move on, it's shark free and if you don't get it finished today you'll be first for the sewer search tomorrow.'
Bruce jokes, 'And I thought my wife was heartless.'
Mac, quick as a flash replies. 'She is.'
Bruce then walks to another part of the jetty.

Bob Evans, 32, who doesn't look English and one of the youngest members of the team, helps Mac on with the rest of his equipment and walks with him to the edge of the jetty. Mac enters the murky water and signals ok by making an O with his thumb and finger as he descends under the surface. Bob feeds out Mac's lifeline as he moves underwater.

Mac begins to feel, and search around the structure of the jetty, visibility is about 25 centimetres. Suddenly and without warning his full-face mask starts to free flow. The noise of the escaping high-pressure air is deafening and to the untrained can cause panic.
Mac has been trained to cope with such an emergency and calmly surfaces to sort out the problem.

On seeing Mac surface Bob shouts to make himself heard above the escaping air, 'Is there a problem?'
'Not sure! No it's working fine.'
Bob jokes, 'A bit dry from last night?'
'I never drink and dive officer.'

Mac adjusts his mask and descends into the water. He is concerned with the air coming from his mouthpiece, and it seems intermittent. Mac continues his search when suddenly the air shuts off completely. He instinctively pulls his reserve button, still no air. Now surfacing is of major importance and as quick as possible. Pushing his suit inflation button he shoots to the surface and hits it like a Polaris missile, pulling off his mask and gasping for air.

Bob shouts, 'What the hell's wrong now?'
Mac, still gasping for air and having swallowed some of the dock water shouts in anger, 'Bloody equipment, I'm getting no air at all now.'
Bob pulls Mac in with the lifeline and helps him out the water. Mac looks at the content's gauge. 'There is plenty of air in the tanks.'
Bob takes the mask and contents gauge from Mac, presses the free flow button on the valve and the air flows freely.
'Sounds perfect to me Mac.'
Mac shakes his head. 'No, something wrong with it mate.' He takes it back and places the mouthpiece in his mouth, breathes in, and air flows.
'Obviously doesn't like the Dock,' Bob replies with a smile on his face.
'Who does? I'll change it for the spare one.'
Bob quickly takes the diving valve from Mac saying, 'I'll get it; you get another tank of air so you have enough to complete the search.'

Bob returns with another diving valve and connects it to the new tank of air. The mask is tested before Mac puts it on; it appears to be working perfectly. Mac gives the ok signal to Bob and descends into the murky water of the Docks.

It only seems like a minute when Bob receives a tug on the lifeline, he counts the pulls, one, two, three, four then five.
'Shit, it's the emergency signal.'
Bob pulls at a frantic pace to get Mac to the surface quickly.

On the surface, Mac rips off his mask and once again gasps for air, and as he is doing so Bob pulls him to the ladder that is attached to the dock wall. 'You OK?'
Mac is coughing, and spitting. 'I'll live. This one is worse than the other one!'
'It can't be?'
Mac is now on the jetty looking really pissed off. Bob has the mask in his hands. He presses the air release purge button, and again the air flows freely. 'I don't understand it's working perfectly,' Bob states with authority.
Seeing Mac is out of the water Sergeant Tony Hayes comes over. 'Have you finished your section already Mac?'
Mac quickly replies, 'No there seems to be a problem with the airflow on these valves I've been using.'
'Use the spare valve.'
'This IS the spare one.' Bob mentions.
Tony turns to Mac. 'How much have you got left to search?'
Mac replies, 'Done about three quarters on this section, but there is still D section to do.'
'Pushing bloody time again.' says Tony.
'I think Bruce has nearly finished; lover boy is going to love you.'

As Tony walks away, he continues, 'See if you can get the diving valve sorted out. If not let me know.'
Mac is now standing between the dive lorry and the end of the jetty and has the spare diving valve in his hands. He watches Bruce go down the ladder to the area he should have finished. Bruce gives the OK sign to his surface buddy, then sees Mac and before descending, gives Mac a wanker sign with his hand.
As Bruce disappears under the water Bob walks over to the lorry.
'Mac, where's the other diving valve?'
'I left it on the jetty.'
Bob looks over to the edge of the jetty and spots the valve. Mac, being closer to the valve shouts, 'I'll get it, you make the tea, and one sugar this time.'

Mac walks towards the valve, picks it up, and suddenly there is an almighty bang. The jetty shudders and the section where Bruce and his buddy are diving explodes, with wood and metal being thrown in the air, and with a flash of flames and smoke. Mac is blown backwards with the force of the explosion. There is utter chaos as other divers start to surface, some holding their ears, suffering from burst eardrums.

All the other personnel involved in the security search congregate to the now smoking jetty. Some of them are giving first aid to diving personnel, others putting out parts of the burning jetty. Mac's dry suit is severely burnt, and he is lying on the jetty receiving medical treatment.

Still in a daze, Mac realizes what has happened and shouts, 'Bruce, Bruce, someone get to Bruce.'

A paramedic kneels by his side. 'There's been an explosion Mr. Mackenzie, you're going to be alright, try not to speak, just relax while we cut your suit off.'

Chapter 2

Who to Blame

The present

Mac is suddenly awakened from his day dreaming by brake lights in front of him.
He is at the wheel of his motor caravan.
There is a road sign he can see ahead of him, and it reads Exeter 90 miles.

Mac pulls off the main road at the next junction, into a country lane. After about 20 minutes driving, he can see a deserted lay-by. The sun is setting and the countryside around him looks stunning.
Turning the engine off, he climbs into the back of the motor caravan. He finds a bottle of whisky in one of the cupboards and pours himself a large one; he then reaches for his sketch-pad and starts to draw.
As he sketches the countryside around him, he pauses for a while and looks at his badly scarred forearm, which is a constant reminder of the past.
With the tiredness of the drive and a large whisky, Mac drifts into a sleep. He is woken by a clap of thunder, which rocks the motor caravan. Looking out of the window he can see heavy rain is now falling and the noise of the raindrops in the caravan is deafening.
Mac looks at the scar on his arm again and his mind drifts back to his past.

Flash back

Chief Superintendent Brian Samways is a man of 50; grey haired and very English, who gives the impression he has done it all before and nothing can shock him. It's raining outside his office, and he is on the telephone.
As he looks out of the window at the River Thames, he can see police boats coming and going from the floating jetty attached to the Police Station.
'There's been a little bother at City Airport. It's mayhem here.'
There is a knock at his door.
'Come in – look I have to go… Yes… as soon as I know myself I'll be in touch, good bye.'

As Superintendent Samways puts down the phone, Inspector Phil Johns, 45 years old, enters his office. Phil is a weasel like man with a pious superior air about him. He has an irritating habit of rubbing his hands as he speaks.
'Ah Phil sit down, what a bloody mess, what the hell happened out there?'
Phil responds eagerly, rubbing his hands, like Fagan in Oliver Twist.
'At the moment we're not sure, but obviously it was intended for our visitor Carlos.'
'Anyone claimed responsibility?'
Still rubbing his hands together, Phil replies. 'Apart from the usual crank calls nothing yet sir.'

A woman police officer enters the office.
'It's about to start sir.'
'Thank you.'
Brian walks over to the television and turns on the news channel.
'Damn News chaps they know too much too bloody quickly.'
The theme tune for the six o'clock news is heard.
A newsreader announces, 'An explosion killed three officers at London City Airport this afternoon, just hours before the arrival of Carlos Azeglio, the Italian right wing extremist Politician, who was due to give a talk in the Guildhall in London'.
Brian walks over and turns the television sound down.
'MI5 and the press will be circling like vultures on this one, I want you to be careful how you tread Phil.'

The woman police officer comes into Brian's office again.
'They're here sir.'
Brian turns to Inspector Phil Johns.
'More press, have you noticed how these things happen on a Friday afternoon, so much for POETS day?'
Phil, (still rubbing his hands), 'They've learnt it gets them more coverage than during the week sir.'
Brian now bored with Phil walks him to the door.
'I don't like surprises: never have, never will. The press will make this a showpiece; don't miss anything on this one, because they won't, Phil.'
'No Sir.'

The Present

Mac wakes up in his motor caravan with the rain still beating down on the roof. He has a stiff neck and decides to have a shower and a shave to wake himself up. After making a cup of tea he reaches for a road map.

Sitting in the driver's seat, he establishes his next route, and quickly finishes his tea before starting the engine of the motor caravan. Mac puts the gear stick into first gear to pull away and nothing happens. He revs the engine, still nothing.

Thinking the clutch has gone, and he will be stuck there for a while, he stares into the windscreen and once again his mind drifts.

Flashback

Forbes Mackenzie, Mac's older brother, 47 years old and slightly overweight, looking like the archetypal detective that he is, is chasing (unsuccessfully) a young lad in his teens down a narrow docklands street.

The boy has begun to tease Forbes by letting him get close then running off. 'You fat pig.' shouts the young lad.

Forbes stops, breathing heavily and very, very out of breath and in anger shouts, 'Your cards are marked, sonny.'

'In your dreams, copper.' The lad shouts back.

The young lad then disappears around a street corner.

Forbes walks back to his car, coughing and still out of breath.

A fellow detective is in the car talking into a police radio, he replaces the radio as Forbes approaches. 'Little turd got away, what did they want?'

'There's been an explosion at City Airport. It's your brother, he's been hurt.'

In a hospital room Mac is sitting up in bed, his face is covered in cuts and bruises, his hands are heavily bandaged.

The TV is on and he is watching the news.

There's a picture of Bruce on the screen.

'Bruce Fraser, 35, was named as one of the three officers killed at City Airport. He had been in the Police Force for twelve years and was considered to be one of the most experienced police divers in the country.'

Forbes Mackenzie enters his brother's hospital room as the announcement on television is being made.
'Hi Forbes turn it off will you?'
Forbes turns the television off and asks Mac, 'Do you need anything?'
Mac stares at the blank TV and starts to cry, something he's never been used to doing. 'No.' He mutters.
Sergeant Tony Hayes enters Mac's room. 'Forbes.'
Forbes nods his head.

Tony looks at Mac and gritting his teeth, says, 'God you're a mess. At least you're alive; we thought they'd got you too at one stage.'
'Mr. Lucky is my middle name, who was the third one Tony?'
'Chris I'm afraid to say.'

Tears began to roll down Mac's cheeks; he tries hard not to cry out loud, biting his tongue to keep his emotions inside. He chokes out,
'It should have been me.'
Tony leaves Mac and Forbes, 'Hope to see you back on your feet soon Mac, the rest of the lads sent their best.'

Forbes makes his excuses to Mac and leaves as well.
He catches Tony up in the hospital corridor. 'What was all that about?'
'Bruce was diving for Mac.'
'How come?'
'Mac was having problems with his breathing equipment, Bruce volunteered to help him out and bang.' Tony states bluntly.
'Was he married?'
'Yes, and a kid, Chris had a little boy, and Mick one on the way.'
'Who did it?'
'We don't know and what's worse we're never going to get them.'

Present Time

Mac blinks, he is back in his motor caravan. He steps outside to inspect it and to his horror finds the van has been bricked up, and all the wheels have been stolen.

He walks round to the back and to his relief the motorbike is still there. Mac climbs back into the van and picks up his car phone and dials a number.
As it rings and rings Mac's mind drifts back to the past again.

Flashback

At the entrance to the police station the press men and photographers are hampering Inspector Phil Johns getting to his car.
Someone shouts. 'Is it true you were given prior warning of the bomb?'
A pressman blocks the car door from closing. Phil goes to push him aside. 'Excuse me.'
The pressman, standing his ground asks, 'Are we looking at more police incompetence?'
Phil ignores the question. 'Excuse me.'
The man moves to one side.
'Thank You.'
Phil gets into the car that is being driven by a young PC who has become Phil's accompanying partner. The PC is almost a carbon copy of his boss, and together they are a slightly menacing team.
The PC goes by the nickname Dipper, which has something to do with an incident he was involved with in his rather cloudy past.

'Morning Sir.'
Phil replies with a big sigh.
'Morning Dipper, get me out of here fast.'

On the jetty near City Airport where the explosion took place, photographs are being taken of the area destroyed by the bomb.
Phil Johns' car arrives.
As the car pulls up near the jetty, Dipper rushes around to open the door for Phil. 'It will be a year before they get this place right sir.'
'Yes Dipper, who says were not at war?'

A forensic officer approaches. 'Good morning Phil.'
Phil replies sarcastically, 'Plenty of overtime for you lot here.'
The forensic officer, sharp as a razor replies, 'I've got overtime into the next century providing we're not rushed, after all we don't want to MISS something do we Phil?'
'You're not going to keep us hanging around for a report on this one are you?'

'I'll do my best. I want to show you something, and keep that police mind of yours busy.'

Present time

Mac's attention is suddenly taken away from his thoughts when someone answers the phone he is holding to his ear. It's the Automobile Association. Mac explains the problem and they tell him they will contact a local garage to come out to him.
They tell him it will take 30 to 40 minutes.
An hour later Mac can see a small pick- up truck pull in front of his motor caravan.

Keith Rembridge, is a man of about 47, his weather-beaten face can't hide the cheeky grin. His accent is very rural, but not strong.
On the side of his truck is written 'Keith Rembridge Tyres'.
'I was beginning to think you'd given up on me.'
' I've given up on a lot of things in my life, but not my customers.' Keith replies, with a huge grin on his face.
He begins to look around Mac's van.
'Erm… You be right there, you won't get far without wheels, I did hear of a man that drove a hundred miles on a flat tyre, mind you, he had three others.'
Keith walks back to his truck scratching his chin.
Mac shouts, 'Do you need a hand?'
'Thanks, but no thanks, but if you got a cup of tea somewhere in that there monster van of yours it wouldn't go amiss.'
Mac steps into the motor caravan and lights the gas under the already full kettle.
While waiting for it to boil, his mind drifts back to his past.

Flash back

There is a small house in the suburbs of South London.
The house is neat and tidy. There is a knock at the door.
A young woman appears. She herself is neat and tidy, it's Bob's wife.

As she opens the door, she is greeted by Inspector Phil Johns and his sidekick, Dipper.

Phil smiles and greets her saying, 'Good morning, is your husband home?'
Bob is sitting in the front room and hears Phil's voice.
He shouts, 'Hello Sir, come in.'
Bob has some small cuts and bruises to his face.
Bob's wife steps aside and allows Phil and Dipper to go through to the front room.
Phil asks, 'How are you feeling?'
'Glad to be alive, Sir.'
'If you need to talk Bob, we can arrange for you to see someone, all in the strictest confidence of course.'
'Thank you Sir.'

Bob's wife enters the room. 'Can I get you anything?'
'No thank you.'
Bob gives his wife a friendly smile, and she leaves the room, and Dipper shuts the door behind her.
Phil and Dipper sit down.
Phil asks, 'While things are fresh in your mind Bob, I need to ask you some questions.'
'I understand.'
'Good. Why was Bruce Fraser diving in your section?'
'We were doing our search when Mac complained that his DV wasn't working properly, this put us behind and Bruce was asked to take over.'

Present time

There's a whistling noise and Mac realises the kettle is boiling.
At the same time, Keith is at the door of the motor caravan, holding a bill in his dirty black hands.
'Can I come in?'
'Yes of course what good timing the kettle has just boiled.'
They sit down to drink the tea that Mac has now made and Keith hands Mac the bill.
Mac looks at it and chokes on his tea. 'Is this right?'
'I'm afraid so Mr. Mackenzie.'
'I thought Dick Turpin wore a mask!'
Mac reaches into a drawer and takes a chequebook out.
'Sorry Mr. Rembridge I haven't got much cash, will a cheque do?'
'Oh, call me Keith please, I hate being formal, and of course a cheque will do, you seem to have a trustworthy face. That will be the price

for all of them tyres; of course if they had only stolen one it would be cheaper.'
Mac, with a sigh replies, 'Of course, Keith, of course.'

Keith spots diving equipment on the floor and asks, 'Come for the wreck diving have you?'
'I do a little bit, yes.'
'Apparently there are a couple of world war two boats out there, they reckon they still got some live bombs on them they do.'
Mac smiles and hands Keith the cheque.
'Thank you.'
Keith shakes Mac's hand in appreciation. 'Glad I could help you out.'
Mac follows Keith outside to his pick up truck.
'Good luck with the rest of your holiday. I'd get some wheel locks for them there wheels if I was you.'
'I'll do that, thanks again.'
Keith gets into his truck, waves goodbye, drives a few yards, stops and shouts, 'Remember them there bombs.'

Mac watches Keith's truck disappear and has another flashback.

<u>Flash back</u>

It's the jetty at City Airport, after the explosion, and he is lying on the floor.
He is clutching the second DV and air hose.
The blast from the explosion has melted the DV and facemask to Mac's hands.

Tthe police station forensic room.
Inspector Phil Johns and Dipper and Bob are there.
A forensic officer enters with the police diver's DV, he hands it to Bob.
Bob demonstrates as he talks. 'The first stage we attach to the air cylinder. These are your contents reading on the depth gauge and this is the mouth piece that you breathe from called the second stage where the pressure of the air is regulated to the same pressure of the water at whatever depth you may be at, this is where Mac thought the fault was sir.'
'And it was the same with both sets?'

'When I checked them, they had a good air flow, but that was on the surface.'
'On both sets?'
'Yes.'
Phil turns to the forensic officer. ' I want to know what is wrong with this?'
'This particular one, nothing, Mac's DV and the spare one were destroyed in the explosion.'
Phil turns to Bob. 'So what was wrong with…?'
Bob interrupts before Phil has finished. 'That's a good question sir.'
Phil looks back at the forensic officer with questioning eyes, waiting for him to say something.
'I don't think we are ever going to know.'
Phil turns to Dipper with a frown on his face.
'This doesn't make me happy.'

Dipper is now driving inspector Johns away from the lab.
Phil is frantically searching through his papers and says, 'Mac had searched half of C section when Bruce volunteered to finish off.'
Dipper Butts in. 'Didn't Mac say he'd searched three quarters?'
'You're right, he did Dipper.'
Dipper has a smug smile on his face.
Looking very thoughtful Phil studies a map of City Airport docks.

Chapter 3

At The Hospital

Flashback

Inspector Phil Johns and Dipper enter Mac's hospital room.
'Morning Sir, forgive me if I don't shake your hand.'
'How are they?'
'They're talking about skin grafts, but I suppose in the circumstances I got off lightly.'
There is a look between Phil and Dipper that Mac notices but does not like. Phil asks, with a false smile, 'How do you feel about answering a few questions?'
Mac, suspicious of Phil's motives, answers, 'Is this official?'
'At this point no, but it will be. What I'm looking for is to get an overall picture of the situation, and to make sure everything our end was done according to Health and Safety procedures.'
Mac, annoyed that Phil should think otherwise says abruptly, 'Fine.'
And Phil, just as abrupt, 'Good.'
Dipper hands a map to Phil, who puts it in front of Mac. 'I need to know exactly where you were when Bruce took over.'

Present time

Mac's thought brings him back to the present. He is driving his motor caravan into a small town in Devon, called Newton Abbott where it's raining heavily.

Mac parks the motor caravan in the town centre. He is near a picture framing shop. He looks through the window and sees a young girl in her teens behind the counter, and she has a vague likeness to his wife; tall, slim with dark flowing hair and a diamond white smile. As he stares his mind drifts back to the Hospital.

Flash back

In the corridor is Mac's wife, Kay Mackenzie, 40 years old but looking a lot younger. She is tall and slim with long dark brown flowing hair. She has an air of sophistication about her.
It's been raining outside and she is dripping wet.
There is a policeman on duty by Mac's room. 'Evening Mrs. Mackenzie.'
'Hello John, how is he.'
'So so.'
Kay quickly enquires with a smile, 'I bet he's grumpy?'
The PC smiles back, and opens the door to Mac's room for Kay.
Kay sees Mac is asleep. She leans over and kisses him on the lips.
Mac wakes and Kay greets him with a smile saying, 'Hi darling.'
Mac slowly moves himself more upright in the bed. 'A friendly face in the storm. . How's Chris's wife?'
'I can't get through, keep getting engaged tone.'
'And the others?'
'The same.'
'Chris was only married for a month, I feel awful.'
'It's not your fault Mac.'
'I know, I know, Inspector Von Johns gave me one of his loving visits this afternoon.'
'They'd have to give me something after a visit from him, what did he want?'
'Not sure, doing his job, I suppose.'
With a look of despair Kay replies, 'The Job, argh. I should have listened to my mother and married a solicitor.'
'But they weren't as good looking as me.'
'Tom Baker was.'
'At twenty feet away.'
'Close up he wasn't too bad.'
'You were never close up to Tom Baker; you said you found him boring?'
'I might have done.'
Mac gives Kay a stern look.
Kay runs her hand under the bed-clothes, and a smile appears on Mac's face.
Kay says laughing, 'Not forgotten how to smile then?' She removes her hand saying, 'Well let's see more of it then.'

Present time

Mac is brought back to the present by a sudden clap of thunder; he quickly enters the framing shop looking like a drowned rat.
'I'm drenched.'
The shop girl, called Charlotte, laughs and replies, 'That's what happens if you stand in the rain, why didn't you come straight in?'
'Oh, my mind was on other things, but I'll remember that.'
'Can I help you?'
'I was wondering if I could have this framed by the end of today.'
Mac produces a painting on canvas of a diver in full dress, sitting in a police boat with Tower Bridge in the background. It's a self-portrait showing him and all the old equipment they used when he first joined the Diving Unit.
'I think it's too late now, but I'll ask.'
Charlotte exits to a room behind the counter. Mac looks around the shop at some framed pictures on the wall. He focuses on one, a can of Coca-cola.
Charlotte returns and says, 'Sorry we can't do the picture until tomorrow.'
'You can have that one you're looking at if you want.'
'Er....thanks, but no thanks, it's not for me.'
'We sell three a week.'
They both stare at the picture.
Charlotte continues, 'every week.'
Charlotte leaves Mac to carry on looking around the shop and we go back to the past.

Flash Back

At the City Airport jetty, Inspector Phil Johns, Dipper and Bob are by the water's edge.
'A difficult search?' enquires Phil.
'It's never easy, it's usually cold, visibility is bad and there's always something unexpected to bump into and get caught up on, but it's shark free.'
'Huh, what shark in its right mind would swim in this open sewer?'
Phil begins to slowly lose his friendly tone. 'But the jetty here is fairly protected?' He looks at his notes and continues, 'and on the day there was no boating traffic, so the water would have been reasonably clear.'

Phil turns to Dipper who has that smug look on his face that always seems to appear when anyone else is in trouble.
'That Friday wasn't cold was it Dipper?'
'No it was quite reasonable for the time of year sir.'
'How deep was the dive?'
Bob intercedes. 'About three metres.'
'Three metres, with Mac's experience a routine straightforward job and no big fish to bother him.'
Bob replies in Mac's defence. 'He's a good instinctive diver, and if he said there was a problem with his DV, then I believe him.'
Phil, not really convinced, replies, 'Having trouble breathing, it's going to be a distraction isn't it?'
There's a silent pause.
'Mr. Evans I asked you a question.'
'I don't know, I wasn't in the water with him.'
Phil's voice lowers and in a calmer voice. 'An unfair question, I apologise.'

In Mac's hospital room, he is sitting up in bed, struggling to turn a page in his newspaper. Mac's hands are still heavily bandaged.
Bob appears at the door. He watches Mac's struggle for a moment and with a smile on his face says, 'I bet wiping your arse is a problem?'
Bob enters Mac's room and sits at the end of the bed.
'I thought you'd forgotten about me?'
'I had to answer a few questions before they'd let me come and see you.'
'Nothing broken then?'
'A few cuts and bruises, that's all.'
Bob nods and looks towards Mac's hands. 'How are they?'
'I'm not out of trouble with them yet, but it's looking better.'
'We both had a lucky escape.'
'I know. How's everyone else?'
'Still in shock, which is not helped by Johns and his stupid questions?'
'Well, he is employed to cover the situation and come up with some answers.'
'I'm not sure. I don't like his attitude, he is a born again who is power mad and wants to get a big promotion, I'd be really careful with him.'
Mac looks at Bob thoughtfully, and then replies, 'It seems a rash statement to make.'

Bob changes the subject saying, 'When are they going to let you out to play then?'
'In a few week's hopefully.'
A Doctor arrives with a nurse. Bob gets up from the end of the bed and gives Mac the diver's OK sign. 'See you soon. Be good, there are some attractive looking nurses in this hospital.'
Bob leaves giving the nurse a smile and a wink.
The Doctor looks at Mac's progress chart.
'How are you feeling Mr. Mackenzie?'
'As well as can be expected.'
'Ok. I will get the nurse to put some smaller bandages on those hands, and we will take you down to have some physiotherapy.'

Mac is now in a what looks like a small gym, he is alone and being put through some exercises by a young doctor whose manner is a bit sharp and short. Mac's hands are bandaged, with his thumb separate from the rest of his fingers, and is able to use it better than before.
His face is now less marked, and the bruises and cuts have started to heal.
Mac is walking on a treadmill and there is a breathing pipe attached to his mouth. Electrodes are attached to his chest, checking his heart rate.
The doctor, holding a clipboard and pen asks, 'How are you feeling?'
Mac thinks to himself, 'The dentist always asks the same sort of thing when you have a mouth full of metal.' He gestures with his thumb that he is fine.
The doctor in a sharp voice continues, 'Try not to let it play on your mind; it will affect the healing of your hands!'
Mac gives the thumbs up sign again.
'Good, could we speed up the pace a bit?'
Mac nods and begins to jog slowly.

Mac is now back in his hospital room and Phil Johns and Dipper have turned up. Phil is speaking to Mac's doctor.
'He could do with losing a few pounds, but physically he is in good shape, emotionally at this point, debatable.'
The doctor's pager sounds. 'If you will excuse me, I have an emergency coming in.'
Phil follows the doctor down the corridor asking, 'Doctor, can you tell me if there are any signs of respiratory disorder?'
'If you mean was the man fit to dive then the answer is yes, Sergeant.'
'It's Inspector, and I'm glad to hear that.'

'If you will excuse me, Inspector, I do have an emergency to attend to.'

Present time

Mac is in Newton Abbott.
He leaves the frame shop and begins to browse through the shops in the town, and is happy and relaxed, the rain has stopped and the sun is out. He reaches a pub and enters for a drink, thinking it's been a while since he tasted Devon's cider.
There are just a few customers in the pub, most looking like they are dressed for farming. Mac orders a pint of scrumpy, which is a strong Devon cider, only for experienced cider drinkers.
He takes his coat off and sits in a corner of the pub on his own.
After a few gulps of the cider Mac feels well relaxed and thinks back to the local pub he frequented when he was in the unit.

Flash back

It's a Thursday evening, the night before the explosion and Mac and other members of the diving team are in the Swan and Cuckoo pub in Wapping. The full diving team, except Bruce, is having a drink to celebrate Chris's birthday. Mac, John, Smoothy and Bob are at one end of the bar, while Chris, Tony, Mike and Lee can be seen at the far end. The pub is busy and buzzing.
Feeling he has had enough now Mac asks Smoothy, 'What time is it?'
'We've got about five minutes before closing.'
John asks, 'Mac what do you want?'
'Same again please John.'
John points to Smoothy's glass.
'Stick a half in there will you. Where's Bruce tonight Mac?'
'No idea, he said he'd be here.'
John hands Mac a pint of bitter.
'Thanks.'
'Bruce never seems to come out for a drink anymore.'
John gives Smoothy his half.
'Cheers John, I think he's got problems at home.'
Mac agrees. 'I think you might be right.'
Bob enters the pub and shouts, 'It's time, let's do it.'

Mac, John, Smoothy and Bob walk over to Chris, Tony, Mike and Lee. There is a friendly scuffle, and they handcuff Chris to the bar.
A woman dressed as a police officer walks into the pub. She walks up to Chris and gives him a long lingering kiss full on the lips.
The pub crowd cheer.
The girl then pulls back and says in a sexy voice, 'Happy Birthday big boy.'
She begins to tease him a little as she slowly takes off her uniform.
She stops, gives him a kiss and walks out.
Chris shouts, 'Oh no, come back, I love you, I want your babies.'
As she disappears out of the door she is replaced by a muscled man, dressed in tight skimpy leathers, and a leather cap.
He walks towards Chris and blows him a kiss.
Chris shouts, 'You Ba…tards.'
The man comes close to Chris and says, 'Happy Birthday big boy.'
He kisses Chris and a photo is taken by one of the diving team.

In a quiet suburb of South London, we are in the lounge of Mac's home. The house is not too different from his present home, the motor caravan. The style is a classical look; the atmosphere is light and airy. There are some framed paintings of Mac's work, one of which can be recognised from one now in his motor caravan.
Mac opens the CD player, but drops the CD on the floor.
His bandaged fingers and hands make it difficult for him to pick it up.
Mac's wife Kay comes into the lounge, she is smartly dressed and says, 'Here let me do it darling.'
Mac is annoyed at his disability and irritated, replies, 'Leave it, I can manage.'
Kay reaches for the CD.
'If I need any help I'll ask.'
Mac tries repeatedly, but cannot pick up the CD. 'Fuckin' useless hands.'
Kay picks it up for him.
'Sorry.'
'I don't know why I put up with you.'
'It's because I'm a hunk of burning love.'
'Oh yes, where?'
Mac takes the CD from Kay and places it into the player and continues, 'here in front of you.'
Mac looks up at Kay and notices, she is done up to the nines and has her expensive perfume on. 'You look nice, where are you going?'
'Nice, I look great. I'm having a drink with Paula.'

'You didn't tell me.'
'There are other things in life apart from you and the police force.'
'Like what?'
'Like me, and I told you this yesterday, where's your mind these days.'
There is a knock at the door.
Kay continues, 'Oh King of the Castle I'll get it.'
Kay walks out to the front door on the way collecting her coat and handbag off the baluster rail, then, opens the door.
'Hi Tony.'
Tony kisses her on the cheek.
'Kay, you look great, off somewhere nice?' Kay winks at Tony.
'He's through there, but be careful, he's snapping like a crocodile.'
Mac shouts, 'Who is it?'
'It's Tony, I'll see you later, bye bye.'
Tony smiles. 'Bye Kay.'

Mac shouts to Tony, 'There should be a couple of beers in the fridge.'
Tony goes into the kitchen and finds two cans of larger in the fridge. He opens the cans and takes them into the lounge and passes one to Mac.
Tony raises his can. 'Cheers.'
'Cheers Tony. Here's to being normal again.'
'What's it like being at home for a change?'
'Better than the hospital, but I'm the outdoor man, it will be good to get back to work and blow a few cobwebs out.'
'I'll bet Kay's never seen so much of you?'
'I think I'm driving her mad.'
'I doubt it. About tomorrow, Lisa's having trouble understanding why you were lucky and why Chris wasn't.'
Mac gives a big sigh. 'I've asked myself the same question repeatedly.'
'Look, if she's a little unfriendly, just remember it's not you, it's the situation and everything.'
'Thanks, how's Bruce's wife?'
She's like everyone else, can't believe it's happened.'
'Apparently things at home were not too good, he'd moved out for some time before the explosion happened.'
'He kept that quiet.'
'Didn't he just.'

Present time

Mac has just finished a pub lunch, but is drinking coffee not alcohol. As he finishes his drink and walks past a church on his way back to the motor caravan, he thinks about the Church where the funerals of his colleagues took place.

Chapter 4

The Funeral

Flash back

The Church is beginning to fill up. Members of the dive team are there with wives and children. Mac is in police uniform and Kay is by his side, and as usual dressed to stand out from the crowd. His hands are still bandaged, and Kay holds them gently.
Chris's wife Lisa, 30 years old, petite, with a slight Mediterranean look and big brown eyes, sits holding the hand of her younger daughter Bethany. John is by her side with a comforting arm around her shoulder. Lisa looks around at the people entering the church. She catches Mac's eye and he smiles at her.
Lisa frowns and turns away to ignore him.

Lisa turns to John and in a voice loud enough for Mac to hear and says, 'What's that bastard doing here?'
John replies in a whisper, 'Lisa this is not the time or the place, please.'
'Isn't it? If he'd done his job none of this would have happened.'
Lisa begins to cry. John tries to comfort her by putting his arm around her shoulder again.
The vicar now in the pulpit starts to speak.
'The loss of any life is a tragic occurrence. Yet when three people in the prime of their lives are taken away from us in this most vicious manner, we must all look deeper within ourselves to forgive those who commit these crimes.'

As the funeral comes to an end, Tony, who is sitting next to Mac asks, 'How is it going?'
'Hopefully the first skin graft will be next month.'
'What then?'
Kay then butts into the conversation, saying, 'Then he can go back to work and get out of my hair.'
John and Smoothy walk past. Mac tries to be friendly and says, 'I've been trying to remain in touch with you, John.'
John and Smoothy ignore him and keep walking.
Mac doesn't give up and shouts. 'John! Smoothy!'

John turns around with a face like thunder. 'I'll say something for you, you've got some nerve coming here today.'
'What are you talking about?'
'We all know you bloody missed it, didn't you, why don't you be man enough to own up to it.'
'I didn't miss anything.'
John replies in a very sarcastic tone, 'Oh of course you didn't, we all thought we'd dress up in black to come here for a laugh. I always thought there was more to you.'
John turns to leave the church, but Mac gets up and puts his arm in front of him. 'John I didn't miss anything, honest.'
John over-reacts at Mac stopping him with his arm and a scuffle breaks out, which is quickly stopped by Bob and Tony pulling John off Mac.
Mac's shirt is ripped and there is blood coming from his lip.
Tony shouts, 'Oi, come on you two, remember where you are.'
John struggles to free himself from Bob and Tony's hold. 'Let go, Tony let go, he started this.'
Bob and Tony let go of John, and he walks away unconcerned about Mac sitting on the floor, shocked and his hands bleeding through the bandages.

Lisa is now seated in the back of a car holding her young daughter Bethany. John is in the front Passenger seat staring out of the window with a glazed look on his face.
Lisa cries out. 'It's not fair; Chris didn't deserve to be killed.'
Smoothy opens the driver's door and sits behind the wheel.
'You ok John?'
'Yes I'll live.'
Lisa shouts from the back seat in anger. 'I want that bastard to suffer John.'
Smoothy starts the car up saying, 'come on its time to move on to the Crematorium.'
Lisa continues, 'John, promise me you'll stitch him up?'
Smoothy looks over at John, and then drives off.
Lisa puts her hand on Johns shoulder saying, 'Chris would have done it for you.'
John and Smoothy look at each other again. 'We'll sort it Lisa. Smoothy come on, and let's get this over with.'

In a stairway of a police station, Chief Superintendent Brian Samways is accompanied by a woman police officer. They are walking down the stairs.

The WPC is in conversation with the Chief Superintendent. 'You need to be back for four and Baker will be over tomorrow morning.'
'Did Baker finish the field case?'
'Yes sir.'
Inspector Phil Johns and PC Dipper are walking up the stairs and meet Chief Superintendent Samways. 'Morning Sir.'
'Phil I understand there was a problem at the church.'
'It would appear that good news travels fast.'
Turning to the WPC Chief Superintendent Samways says, 'That will be all for now, I'll see you in my office at one.'
The WPC smiles and winks at Chief Superintendent Samways.
He waits until the WPC is out of earshot and continues, 'what did forensic say Phil?'
'They're not sure and they are not going to commit themselves too early, it's going to be another week before we know anything.'
Samways in a low voice, almost a whisper, says, 'What do you think?'
There is a silent pause. Samways looking at Dipper, says in a whisper, 'Between us?'
Phil whisper back, his mouth to Samways' ear, 'He missed it and he knows he did.'
'And the breathing apparatus?'
'Both sets have been destroyed, and at this point I'm not sure if it's good news for us or it's some ace up his sleeve for him.'
The WPC returns. 'Sir, the car is waiting for you.'
'The delay by forensic might be useful. Make sure he doesn't have any skeletons in his cupboard, and Phil, good work.'
'Thank you Sir.'
Phil continues up the stairs to his office, he sees John and Smoothy outside. 'Yes gentlemen what can I do for you?'
Smoothy speaks up. 'Sir, we would like to have a word about William Mackenzie.'
'You better come into my office then.'
Dipper also follows them in and remains standing, notebook in hand, while they take a seat the other side of Phil's desk.
John starts the conversation. 'Sir, the night before the search it was Chris's birthday and we, as a unit went out to celebrate, and Mac as usual overdid it with the drink.'
Smoothy pipes up. 'He missed it didn't he Sir?'
Phil leans forward his elbows on the desk.
'The location of the explosives has not been verified, I suggest with such a delicate matter as this, that idle gossip is dangerous and to reserve your judgement until all the evidence is in.'

'I believe he was still drunk when he dived, and it affected his judgement Sir.'
'You and Chris grew up together didn't you Smoothy?'
'I've known him….. knew him…..., since I was 7 years old.'
'It's a very difficult time. Let's forget about this conversation; it's for the best. You both have a re-think and come and see me in a few days.'
There is a silent pause, and then John says, 'With respect Sir, I can't see a few days changing our opinion.

In Mac's Kitchen, he struggles to make a cup of coffee with his bandaged hands and fingers. Tony is there but makes no effort to help him. They have known each other, since they were knee high. He has heard a rumour, and he's gone off the rails.
'You didn't answer my question Tony.'
'These guys are not hillbillies with a few sticks of dynamite and nothing better to do, they're professionals.'
'So am I.'
Tony moves to take over making the coffee, as Mac seems to be taking forever. 'You're making a pig's ear of that. I'll do it before we both die of thirst.'
Mac moves away and lets Tony get on with it. 'You still didn't answer me.'
'I want to believe you Mac, for your sake, I hope you didn't miss it.'

Chapter 5

The Stitch Up

In a car somewhere in London, John and Smoothy are following someone, Smoothy is driving.
John says, 'Stay back.'
'They've turned into Temple Street.'
'Drive past we'll get in from the other side.'
As they drive past, a car turns into a London side street, but it's not clear who the driver is. As John and Smoothy follow the car it pulls up in a quiet street and parks. The lights are turned off but the occupants stay in the car. John and Smoothy park a few yards away.
Smoothy lights up two cigarettes and hands one to John. 'Cheers, here we go.'
'No hang on John, give them time to get at it.'
They wait for fifteen minutes then see movement in the car.
'Ok I think now is a good time; off you go John.'
John gets out of the car with a camera; he can see the couple in the car are in a compromising position. Click, the first flash startles them, and the second captures their startled faces, close together. A few more clicks, and John runs back to the car.
'I think that will do the trick Smoothy.'
John and Smoothy drive off into the night.

In Mac's lounge, he is sitting watching TV and feeling very unhappy.
He hears the front door open, then close. 'Kay, is that you?'
Kay enters the lounge, walks over to Mac and kisses him on the brow. 'Hi darling, how are you feeling?'
'You're late.'
'Ooo, who's rattled your cage?' Kay looks at her watch. 'Oh, 3 minutes late, a definite capital offence, let's call in the firing squad shall we?'
She walks out of the lounge and shouts back. 'You need to get out of the house more, and stop feeling sorry for yourself, I'm going to bed. I'm tired.'
Mac looks at the clock, it shows 10:33pm.

Mac and his brother Forbes arrive at the hospital, it's very busy with doctors and nurses walking up and down the corridor and people hanging around waiting to be seen. After a long wait Mac is called and shown into a medical room where a doctor and nurse are waiting. The doctor tells Mac to sit down and starts to slowly take the bandages off his hands. They are still red and blistered.
'They're getting better Mr. Mackenzie.'
'You could have fooled me.'
'Try and make a fist.'
Mac tries to make a fist but it's tight and painful. As he does so he screws his face up with the pain and effort that are required to make the fist.
The doctor gets some ointment and fresh bandages and says, 'They look far worse than they are, and with a bit of luck you're not going to need skin grafts.'
'Great, when can I start work?'
'The skin will need time to heal, it won't be until round about January before you can even think about any work.'
'What? You are joking I hope?'
'No I'm not Mr. Mackenzie, you must be patient, or you will delay the healing process.'

Forbes is still sitting in the waiting room when he sees Mac come out of the medical room. 'Take a seat Mr. Mackenzie while I get your new painkillers.'
'Thank you Doctor.' Mac sits next to Forbes.
'Well, how are the hands?'
'Do you want the good news or the bad news?'
'Depends if it's going to cost me any money or not.'
'Good news I will be able to start work in about two months.'
And the bad news?'
'Will I have a job to go to?'
'You've been diving for 20 years Mac. If it was down there you would have found it; your record alone shows that, don't you think?'
'Yes.'
Mac is now in the hospital waiting room. The doctor enters the room.
'These tablets should ease the pain and remember to continue the exercise. I'll see you on Thursday morning.'
The doctor leaves and Mac and Forbes are alone in the empty waiting room.
'I've been over the search a million times in my head, it just wasn't there Forbes.'

'Stop feeling sorry for yourself and get it into your head you're going to be a house husband for a while, and when you get bored with that you can come and clean my place and have a beer or two or three.'
'Get some Irish whiskey in, and you're on!'
'You know I've always got a bottle of that in for you.'

In Mac's lounge, he is struggling to put a CD in the hi fi. In a fit of frustration, he throws the CD across the room, gets up and puts on his coat and leaves the house.

It's lunchtime Mac is alone in a bar, he has drunk enough Irish whiskey to sink a battleship. He is drunk, very drunk.
A man walks to the bar, and accidentally knocks Mac's arm as he is swaying on the barstool. 'Sorry mate didn't see you there.'
In a slurred voice Mac replies, 'There, it wasn't there.'
The man can see he is drunk and tries to humour him. 'If it wasn't there mate then that's fine by me.'
Mac stares into his glass of whisky and visualizes his search underwater. 'Another whisky my good man and make it a large one.'
The barman can see Mac has had enough and politely replies, 'Sorry mate, I think you've had enough, now please don't make me have to call the police. Just leave the bar now, please.'
Mac drinks the rest of his whiskey and staggers out of the pub.
On his way out, he sees the man that knocked his arm and shouts. 'Oi, it wasn't there.'

In Mac's house, he is lying on the floor in the hallway. Kay enters through the front door and is startled to see him lying there, thinking he may have injured himself. 'Mac?'
There is no response.
As she bends down next to him, she can smell the whiskey. 'You stupid man Mac, are you trying to kill yourself. Go to bed.'
Mac is dead to the world and there is no way he can make it to his bed. Kay steps over him, hangs her coat up and walks into the kitchen, leaving Mac to sleep it off in the hallway.

In a dark room somewhere in Hounslow, Smoothy and John are developing photographs. John lifts a picture out of a bowl of photographic developing solution. 'What do you think Smoothy?'
' Sexy. David Bailey eat your heart out.'

In Mac and Kay's bedroom Mac is getting dressed. His bandaged hands are hindering his progress. He is less frustrated than he had been in the early stages of the injury, and resigned to the fact that his hands are going to cause him problems for a while longer.

'Sod it; I'm going in a T-shirt.'

With this remark Kay gets out of bed to help him.

Mac kisses his wife then hands her a tie.

'Come on Mac, chin up and all that; don't look so worried.'

'But I am.'

She steps back and puts her hands on her hips. 'If you don't smile I won't help you.'

Mac gives a fake happy smile. Kay then continues to help him get ready. 'They are only going to ask you a few more questions, what's the big deal for God's sake?'

'I've not been much help lately have I?'

With a sigh Kay says, 'we're supposed to help each other that's part of the deal. Are you sure you don't want me to come with you?'

'I'm a big boy now, and anyway they won't let you in.'

The front door bell rings, Mac kisses Kay and says, 'I'll see you later.'

She gives him a hug and whispers, 'Trust me you have nothing to worry about.'

Mac is alone in an interview room at the Police Station. A woman police officer enters. 'They will be with you in a minute Mr. Mackenzie.'

She hands him an envelope. 'This was left at the reception for you.'

'Thank you.'

Mac takes the envelope and opens it with his teeth, and then tips out the contents onto the desk. He reads the first page.

IF YOU TAKE 'A' OFF PAULA, YOU'RE LEFT WITH PAUL.'

As he struggles to turn the next page with his bandaged hands, he sees a photograph of his wife in a compromising position kissing another man.

The woman police officer enters the room again. 'You can go in now.'

Mac's brain is racing and the shock of the photo throws him into a panic, his mind is racing. 'Pardon?'

'It's time to go in Mr. Mackenzie.'

At the same time, Tony walks in. 'Sorry I'm late Mac, the traffic is bloody awful.'

'Oh, um, sorry Tony good to see you.'

'Stop looking so worried you got nothing to fear Mac.'

The woman police officer says again in an impatient voice, 'Please Mr. Mackenzie, they're waiting.'

Inside, Chief Superintendent Brian Samways' office is Inspector Phil Johns, PC Dipper and a WPC, who is taking notes.
Sergeants Mackenzie and Hayes enter the office. They are greeted with a smile from Chief Superintendent Samways. 'I'm pleased to hear there is no permanent damage to your hands Sergeant Mackenzie.'
'Thank you sir, with a bit of luck, I should be back at work around Christmas.'
Samways takes a long look at Mac; there is an awful silent pause before he answers. 'To be candid with you Sergeant Mackenzie, there are some unanswered questions, which are causing us grave concern.'
Mac tries to sound relaxed but his mouth is drying up. 'I'll be happy to help in any way I can.'
Samways replies in a forceful voice. 'Good.'
Inspector Phil Johns interjects.
'Are you familiar with the expression 'beating the valve'?'
'Yes I am.'
'Would you explain it to me?'
'A diver can sometimes breathe faster than the air valve can supply air to him, that's basically it.'
'Causing what effect?'
'You will have trouble breathing underwater, but as long as you don't panic it won't kill you.'
'Is beating the valve a common problem?'
'It usually happens when a diver is tense or apprehensive, if you are experienced...........'
Inspector Johns leans forward and interrupts Mac. 'Would alcohol make someone beat the valve as you say?'
'If they are stupid enough to dive with a hangover it might, yes.'
'I said alcohol, not a hangover.' Inspector Johns leans back in his chair and continues. 'On the day of the explosion did you dive with a hangover Sergeant?'
Mac can't believe how the questioning is going towards accusations against him and gets angry, shouting, 'WHAT! NO. No I didn't and I wasn't beating the valve either. There was a fault with the DV.'

Tony looks at Mac and waves his hand at waist level below the view of the interviewees, indicating to Mac to calm down.
Johns continues. 'On both sets there was a fault?'

'Yes, on both sets.'
Johns now opens a map of City Airport docks. 'The forensic report states the bomb was here.'
He pushes the map across the table to Mac and points with his finger. 'In the first half of section 'C', the section you gave the all clear to!'
This evidence devastates Mac. He clenches his fist hard and blood begins to drip from one of his bandaged fingers. Tony, seeing how this has upset Mac, asks Superintendent Samways to adjourn the interview, and he agrees.

Chapter 6

Total Breakdown

Somewhere in South London a Ford Sierra is being driven erratically along the road. As the car approaches a large roundabout it continues forward until it hits the kerb in the middle of the island.
The reversing lights then come on, and the Sierra deliberately reverses backwards around the roundabout.
It's Mac. He is still wearing the clothes from the interview, although they are now rather dishevelled, and he is drinking from a bottle of whisky as he drives. Mac's bandaged hands are now completely bloodstained. He swings the car around with a handbrake turn and stops.
Looking in front of him, he sees a huge illuminated yellow sign that reads, NCP (National Car Parks). Mac drives toward the sign, and stops outside the entrance to the car park, he gets out of his car and walks towards the sign, for a moment mesmerised by it's brilliance in the night sky. A young car park attendant is sitting in a kiosk below the sign, reading a book.
Mac presses his face up against the kiosk window. 'What ya reading?'
The attendant jumps, and then shows Mac the book cover.
Mac continues in a slurred voice, 'do you want to tell me what happens?'
'No it's alright.'
Mac laughs and says, 'This bloke plants a bomb, and it goes BANG, they all die, ha ha.'
'What do you want mate?'
'A room for the night, single or double I don't mind.'
'You're in a car park mate.'
Mac stares around in a daze. 'What is this place Hotel Colditz?'
Have you got crap in your ears? Watch my lips.' He then slurs in separated words. 'I....Want....a ......room.....for.......the.......night.'
He puts his hands on the window and smears blood everywhere.
The young attendant horrified hits the panic button in the kiosk.
Bells begin to ring. Mac puts his hands over his ears, smearing blood all over his face.
He becomes disorientated and leaves, climbs into his car and drives away.

Two young Policemen are on duty in a police car when they hear their radio send out a message. 'Delta 4, the vehicle in question is registered to a Sergeant William Mackenzie, repeat, Sergeant William Mackenzie. There was a report of blood, so proceed with caution, over.'
'Delta 4 confirmed, over.'
One of the Policemen in the patrol car remarks to his colleague, 'That's the guy from the City Airport explosion. I heard he's a right tosser.'

As they continue their search, they see a car parked up in the distance that matches the description. They pull alongside and one of the PC's shines a torch into the car and can see Mac slumped over the steering wheel. They pull up and park in front of the Sierra.
One PC picks up the radio mike. 'MP this is delta 4, can you re - confirm the registration, over.'
'Delta 4 the registration is Echo 5 6 6 Bravo November Oscar, over.'
'MP to Delta 4 do you require assistance over?'
'Delta 4, Negative, over.'
The two PC's approach Mac's car with caution. One knocks on the car window. 'Mr. Mackenzie, get out of the car please.'
Mac opens his eyes, rolls down the window and smiling says, 'It's the boys in blue come to rescue me?'
The PC, now in a louder voice says, 'Can you step out of the car please?'
Mac slurs, 'Please! Please! First day in the job is it, I'd get your mate to do it, and he looks a lot tougher than you.'
'GET OUT, NOW.'
Mac smiles, and as he gets out of the car and slurs, 'That's more like it Osifer.'
He holds his hands forward to be handcuffed. 'I surrender, it's a fair cop.'
They notice the bandages around his hands are dripping with blood.
Mac is put into the back of the police car and taken back to the police station. At the police station his first request is to use the toilet.
They suggest the bandages on his hands be seen to first and Mac nods in agreement. He seems less drunk now but looks terrible.
The PC's relate the arrest to the duty Sergeant.
'Ok he can have a pee now and you may as well get a sample at the same time.'
The 2 PC's accompany Mac to the cell toilet.

As Mac pees into the sample bottle held by one of the PC's he says, 'I'm sorry boys, I know you've got enough trouble without grown piss heads like me taking up your time.'
The PC takes the bottle away before it overflows. Mac takes a seat in the cell, and they slam and lock the cell door.

Mac's brother Forbes enters the charge room. The duty Sergeant recognises him. 'Cell 5.'
'How is he?'
'Gutted wouldn't be a bad starting point.'
The duty Sergeant hands Forbes a set of cell keys. 'He could probably do with a drink of water. There are some cups in the sink in the first room before the cells.'
Forbes goes into the room the duty Sergeant indicated. As he is filling the cup with water, he sees two urine sample bottles full of urine.
One is marked William Mackenzie.
Forbes leaves the room with the cup of water and continues to cell 5 where he unlocks the door. Mac is wrapped in a blanket as he had all his clothes taken away.
'There's nothing like handing someone a stick to beat you with.'
'I don't need it Forbes; I've got a hangover from hell.'
Forbes hands him the cup of water. 'Here take this you're probably dehydrated.'
'Thanks.'
'Do you want me to call Kay?'
'No.'
'You're the expert on divorce, what's it like?'
'It's crap, trust me. Now what's going on Mac?'
Mac begins to sob uncontrollably.
Forbes is concerned; he has never seen his brother like this.
Mac sobs. 'I don't think I can hold it together anymore Forbes.
I need help.'
Forbes sits beside him and puts him arm around Mac. 'Whatever it is we will sort it out. Meanwhile get some rest, you look awful.'
Forbes leaves and locks the cell door behind him.
He has the empty cup in his hand and looks at it thoughtfully.
He walks back into the room where he got the cup of water and looks at the two urine samples.
Glancing around to make sure no one is looking, he pours the sample marked William Mackenzie down the sink.
The sound of peeing and a zip can be heard from the room.
Forbes returns to the charge room and returns the key to the duty Sergeant. 'Thanks for the phone call; he's sleeping it off now.'

The Sergeant looks at Forbes over his spectacles. 'Remember Forbes you didn't get it from me.'
'You can forget I was ever here, I owe you one.'

Chapter 7

A New Beginning

Flash back

Mac has been admitted to a Hospital somewhere in Epsom. He is alone and engrossed in a drawing. Art has always been a passion of his, and now he has all the time in the world to express himself.
It's a lovely day and he is enjoying his passion in the hospital grounds when Forbes arrives and walks towards him. Aware of a shadow over his drawing Mac looks up. Forbes smiles.
Mac points to what he is drawing. 'What do you think?'
Forbes looks for a while and smiles again. 'I'm impressed.'

A senior nurse walks towards them with a glass of water.
'It's time for your medication Mr Mackenzie.'
Mac takes the pill he is given and washes it down with the glass of water. 'This is my brother Forbes. He is still unfortunate enough to be in the police force.'
The nurse replies. 'What's right for one person is not necessarily good for another.'
She turns to Forbes and extends her hand for a handshake. 'Pleased to meet you.'
Forbes returns the gesture. 'And you, how's he behaving?'
With a cheeky smile, she replies, 'Nothing we can't handle. You're not to excite him now.'
She turns to Mac. 'Mr Mackenzie's dinner will be in half an hour and try not to be too late today.'
As she turns to leave Forbes remarks, 'Lucky you, she's pretty and a true professional.'

Mac closes up his sketchpad and says, 'Now I know how Jack Nicholson felt in 'One Flew Over The Cuckoo's Nest.'
'Do you want to come and stay with me?'
Mac answers quickly and abruptly, 'No thanks I like it here. Come on Forbes, I'll show you around.'
They begin to walk and take in the stunning surroundings. 'This place was built by one of those Victorians, who could do everything. Someone famous, I've never heard of. You've got to admire him, he's got it right.'

Forbes not that impressed with old building replies, 'I prefer the Costa Blanca myself.'
'Do you know that being here officially makes me a loony, no responsibility, all found and time to concentrate on my art, it's great.'
'They could have saved themselves the trouble and asked me if you were nuts.'
Mac looks at Forbes suspiciously. 'Is this a social visit, or have you come to say what I think you are going to say?'
Forbes comes straight to the point. 'Kay wants a divorce.'
'Surprise, surprise.'

They continue walking to an isolated spot and sit on the ground for a rest. Mac turns and looks at Forbes, who is now lying on his back with his eyes closed against the warm sun. 'What happened to that urine sample Forbes?'
Forbes still with his eyes closed raises his eyebrows. 'No idea. I did read that people who are depressed can often look like they are smashed out of their heads.'
Mac sarcastically replies, 'Is that so?'
Forbes answers back, 'So I'm told.' Then, changing the subject, 'Come on you'll be late for dinner, and if you're not scared of her, I am.'
They begin to walk back to the main building.
'What are the women like in this place?'
'Raving bonkers.'

Weeks go by and Mac gets more relaxed being in the Hospital and is at peace with the world. He has had time to paint, read and do some walking around the grounds, and most important of all to think about his future.

The day arrives for Mac to leave the Hospital. He stands outside the entrance with a small suitcase by his feet and a sketchpad under his arm. A car comes up the driveway. It's Forbes and he has come to collect Mac.
As he pulls up to the entrance where Mac is standing, he shouts out the window. 'Are you sure you want to do this?'
Mac gets in the car and fastens his seat belt. 'Yes, absolutely, I've been in here long enough to have the time to think it through.'
As they drive away Forbes says, 'to be honest with you Mac, I think you're mad.'

**'But I've got a piece of paper here saying I'm not, where's yours?'
Trying to change Mac's mind Forbes says, 'Why don't you come and stay with me while you think about it?'
'Mac replies, in a very determined voice, 'I've been thinking about it for the last four months.'
They drive in silence for a while then Forbes says, 'It's a stupid idea.'
'Marriage, mortgage, money, that's all I have been worrying about for the last 20 years, and I've had enough.'**

**Forbes pulls onto a gravel drive and they both get out of the car.
In front of them is a large Winnebago motor caravan. Mac turns and smiles at Forbes who has a frown on his face. He then throws his suitcase into the cab of the Winnebago and climbs into the driver's seat.
Forbes, standing alongside the Winnebago shouts, 'If you get stuck you know where you can get hold of me.'
'I'll send you a postcard and thanks Forbes.'
'Are you sure you're not having a mid life crisis?'
'No, I've got that to come.'
Mac starts up the Winnebago toots the horn and drives off.**

Present time

**Back to present time Mac is in the picture framing shop in Newton Abbott, and it's raining outside. He is standing at the counter, soaking wet. The girl behind the counter smiles and says, 'It's the rain man!'
Mac smiles back. 'I think Tom Cruise has the edge on that one.'
'I don't know about that, get rid of the beard, have a haircut, and you'd look alright, maybe cool even.'
Mac, very flattered replies, 'Me, cool, do you think so?'
'Yea mmm ish.'
She lifts the framed picture of a diver and continues, 'I prefer the can of coke myself.'**

**Mac is now outside a barber shop in Newton Abbott and is looking at his reflection in the shop window, deciding whether to go in or not.
He enters the barbershop, and after half an hour looks at himself in the mirror.**

His hair is shorter and he is now clean-shaven, he then makes a comment to the barber. 'Rain Man!'
'You don't like it?'
'I like it, I like it very much. What do I owe you?'

Some time later Mac is in his Winnebago driving out of Newton Abbott heading east. The finished framed painting of the diver is on the passenger seat. On the dashboard is a bottle of Valium pills.
Mac takes hold of the bottle and unscrews the lid, so he can take some pills. With one hand on the steering wheel and the other holding the bottle he puts it to his mouth to swallow some pills, but changes his mind and throws the lot out of the window.

After driving for an hour Mac arrives at a small seaside town called Exmouth. He drives along a seafront that is busy with people. He drives slowly to take in the view, the beach, the sea and fishing boats going to and fro.
Looking at the children playing on the beach reminds him of his own childhood, when his dad took the family to Exmouth and taught him to swim in the sea. How the whole family spent days of the summer there; Mum bringing a picnic that seemed to have endless food and drink; of fighting with his brothers in the sand pretending they were in the Sahara desert like their father was during World War Two; and picking up razor fish and mussels. He wishes he could turn the clock back to then when there wasn't a care in the world and the only worry was if Mum had any food left.

He continues on into a small housing estate in Exmouth. He drives into a long road with several cul-de-sac roads branching off. The street is full of parked cars, and it is difficult for Mac to manoeuvre his large motor caravan, so he reverses back until he finds a suitable space big enough to park it.

He gets out and locks the door of the Winnebago and starts walking to one of the cul-de-sacs carrying with him a framed picture of a dog.
In a house in one of the cul-de-sacs a knock is heard at the front door. A dog begins to bark and Natasha Downing, one of Mac's daughters, an attractive petite lady, with a round face, big brown eyes and an infectious smile, walks down the hallway to open the door. There is a silent pause as they take each other in, then Natasha screams in delight. 'Dad!'
They hug each other and a small tear appears in Natasha's eye.
'Hello Tash, you look well.'

A long legged mongrel dog comes running into the hall and greets Mac by jumping up and trying to lick his face, at the same time wagging his tail furiously.
'Hello Bella, haven't forgotten me then?'
Mac's son in law Gary Downing, is a tall but stocky man with close-cropped hair, whose manner is older than his years. Gary looks hard but is soft at heart, loves animals and worships the ground Natasha walks on.
'Hello Mac this is a surprise. If I'd know I would have got some whisky in.'
'Yes I know you would; how's work then Gary?'
'Can't complain; still pleased to have a job in this day and age. When are you starting back in the Force ....I mean work?
'Not sure. I'm going to take some time off for now.'
Natasha is looking at the painting of Bella her dog.
'It's different from your usual work, Dad, thank you, I love it.'
She kisses him on the cheek.
Gary turns to look at the painting as well.
'It's very nice, her to a tee.'
'Nice, just nice? Well I think it's great.'
Natasha continues, 'You sounded like Mum then Dad.'
'How is she?'
'She's well, very well. They went to Malta yesterday.'
'Thought they would be fed up with Malta by now?'
Mac looks at his daughter with enquiring eyes. 'But then I suppose it's always been her favourite resort for one reason or another?'
Tash with a knowing look answers, 'Yes Dad.'
Mac looks at his daughter straight in the eye and says with some conviction, 'I was surprised you didn't come and see me in the hospital?'
There's a brief silence, Gary looks at Tash and says, 'I'll go and make some coffee shall I?'
'Please Gary.'
Gary walks out of sight into the kitchen and leaves Mac and Tash alone in the lounge.
'Gary and I approve of Paul, he's a nice kind man. He makes mum happy and when mum comes home from work he's always there to greet her. So I thought it would be best if I didn't come and see you for a while.'
Gary puts his head around the door. 'Sugar Mac?'
'Just one for me thanks Gary.'
Gary returns to the kitchen.

Mac and Natasha sit looking at each other in silence, each waiting for the other to speak.
Mac breaks the silence and smiles. 'Put the coffee on hold for a moment, there is something I want to show you.'
Mac and Tash leave the house, and he takes her down the road, but before they turn the corner he says, 'Close your eyes.'
'What?'
'I said close your eyes and trust me.'
Tash closes her eyes and smiles saying, 'Huh I've heard that one before, and usually it was aimed at Mum.'
Mac leads her around the corner and stops in front of the monster motor caravan. 'What do you think?'
Tash opens her eyes, and then her mouth in astonishment.
'Oh my God, what is it; it's enormous?'
Mac stutters. 'It's.........It's my home.'
Mac opens up the Winnebago and starts showing Tash some of the many gadgets inside.
'Watch this Tash.' Mac grabs a remote control, and switches the TV on and off, then switches the radio on and off and then the lights, and dims them.
With a grin from ear to ear and arms spread Mac announces. 'The complete home, I can take it anywhere in the world.'
Tash looks at her Dad with half a smile.
Mac doesn't know whether she likes it or not or whether she thinks he has completely lost it.
'Well do you like it or not?'
'I can't believe you've bought this monster and are going to live like a gipsy, Mum said that you'd never grow up.'
'Emma, I mean your mum might have been right there Tash.'
'Is that why you shaved your beard off?'
'It's the new me!'
'We liked the old one to be honest.'
'But I didn't and I thought it's time to start afresh.'
They walk back to the house, and Mac says, fishing for compliments, 'so you like this Paul more than you do your own Dad do you?'
'No, don't be so sensitive, Dad, you and Mum never saw each other because of your job, and you'd both been living a lie for too long and she didn't deserve to live that way and neither did you.'
Mac says thoughtfully, 'I wonder if we married too young? I suppose we tried it, and it didn't work out.'
Tash holds his hand and gives it a reassuring squeeze, and changes the subject. 'Are you going to stay tonight?'
'I hope so, if it's ok with you and Gary.'

Now in the house Mac and Tash are standing outside the spare bedroom.
'I'm glad you came to see us Dad, and I'm sorry I didn't come to see you in the hospital.'
Mac looks her in the eye with sincerity saying, 'I love you Tash.'
Tash smiles back and kisses him on the cheek. 'I love you too Dad, and I always will no matter what. Goodnight.'
'Goodnight Tash.'

The following morning Mac, Gary and Natasha are standing by the Winnebago. Tash gives him a hug. 'Good luck Dad and drive carefully.'
Gary shakes Mac hands and says, 'Nice to see you again, I must keep a bottle of whisky in the house in case you pay another surprise visit.'
'Nice.....Nice to see you again Gary.'
Mac then whispers in his daughter's ear.
'Teach him another word apart from nice, like 'good' maybe.'
'I'll see what I can do.'
Mac climbs into his motor- caravan, starts the engine with a roar and drives away. He looks in his rear view mirror and sees Tash wipe a tear from her eye, then puts his hand out the window and waves goodbye.

Mac is soon heading toward Torquay.
Alex Lewis, 29, a fit looking young man with long hair and a much laid back attitude to life runs a diving shop in Torquay. Mac enters the diving shop with his dive tank resting over his shoulder.
Alex greets him. 'Good morning sir, what can I do for you?'
'Hi, I need this tank refilling, can you do it here?'
Alex takes the tank off him and looks at the test date stamped into it.
'Yes, no problem. Come back in an hour, and I'll have it ready.'
'I also want to do some diving in the next few days, can you help me out?'
'I think so; I've got a list here,' Alex hands Mac a piece of paper and continues, 'there's a dive this afternoon if you're interested, but it's for experienced divers only I'm afraid.'
Mac reaches into his coat pocket and pulls out his police divers log book, showing it to Alex.
Alex smiles and says, 'no problem, see you at two and don't be late.'

Chapter 8

Diving for pleasure

Present time

Alex and Mac are on a boat heading out to sea from Torquay harbour. There are a few other divers with them talking to each other. Mac is not involved in the conversation and is helping Alex get the diving equipment ready.
'What's down there then Alex?'
'An old tug. She went down 30 years ago, sunk for insurance money they say.'
Mac replies, with a knowing smile on his face, 'dived a few of those in my time.'
'How's the police force these days?'
'No idea, I've finished with it.'
'Had enough of finding dead bodies, yea?'
'Yes, something like that.'
A man in his early 50's Geoff Lee, tall and fit looking, with a ruddy face, and a square chin, calls Alex. 'Alex, come here a minute will you.'
Alex turns to Mac who is coiling some rope, 'Nearly there.'
Alex moves to the helm of the boat where Geoff is steering.
Geoff whispers, 'I've just twigged, you know whom that be don't you?'
Alex looks at Geoff puzzled. 'No?'
'It's that there pissed police diver who missed the bomb at City airport. I saw his picture in the newspaper.'
Alex turns and looks at Mac and then shouts. 'Ok everyone we're here, get your gear on and start doing your buddy checks.'
Mac's intuition and the whispering and the look Alex gave him, makes him realise he's been recognised. He sits on the edge of the boat but doesn't put his tank on.
Alex asks, 'What's wrong?'
'Look if you don't want me to dive, I won't be offended.'
Alex stands bolt upright and looks at Mac straight in the eye. 'I'm responsible for the dive today and someone of your experience is welcome anytime. There's an odd number, so you can buddy with me, Mac if that makes you happy.'
'Sure does.'
Alex gives the divers a final briefing.

'The tug we are diving on is 30 metres down; I don't want to complicate it by making it a decompression dive so no one stays longer than 25 minutes.'
The divers now all dressed and with equipment checked for safety enter the water one at a time by falling backward into the water.
They all have a good dive, everyone keeping to the 25-minute dive time without incident and eventually return to Torquay.
Back at the dive shop Mac and Alex reflect on the day's dive.
'Thanks for letting me come along. It's been a while since I dived for pleasure.'
'Where in Torquay are you staying?'
With a laugh Mac replies, 'I'm sort of in transit.'
Alex hands Mac a business card. 'That's the number there. If you get bored you're more than welcome anytime, and we'll give you a discount on filling your tank as well.'
'I'll bear that in mind, thanks Alex.'

Mac drives his Winnebago to a secluded spot just outside Torquay, where he remembers courting a young girl in his youth, wondering what happened to her, and if he bumped into her would they recognise each other.
Sitting in his cab he can see the sea and Torquay in the distance. He can just about hear the waves breaking against the harbour wall.
Mac retires to the lounge area of the Winnebago and is painting while listening to the world service on the radio. His hands and arms are covered in paint.
His attention is suddenly drawn to an announcement on the radio.
'This is the 10 o clock news. Amid tight security Carlos Azeglio the Italian right wing politician finally gave his much awaited talk at the Guildhall in London.
His earlier visit had been cancelled when three police divers lost their lives in a bomb attack that was…'
Mac picks up the remote control and turns the radio off. He starts to dwell on the radio announcement and drifts back to the time he was in the police force.

Flashback

Mac remembers a time before the explosion, they are all in the diving unit mess, some are making breakfast, others writing reports.
John is talking with Smoothy. 'I'm thinking of buying a Jag.'
'You're mad.'
Chris looks over and says, 'how can you afford that?'
Mac joins in the conversation. 'That's for him to know and you to wonder.'
An attractive woman enters the mess, Gaynor Evans, 32. She is a civilian working in the police station. Gay, as she is known, has long legs and big breasts and is fancied by most of the men in the station. She is fully aware of this and enjoys the attention.
Gay joins in the conversation and with a smile and in a sexy voice says to John, 'this going to be your passion wagon John?'
John is embarrassed by this remark and turns red in the face.
Gay then turns to Tony, pressing herself close to him and says, 'These are the forms you have to sign.'
Tony almost choking on her strong, cheap, perfume signs the forms and hands them back. Gay leaves the mess with an over exaggerated wiggle of her bum and turns to John and winks.
When she is out of earshot John turns to Chris and says, 'I wouldn't mind getting passionate with her some time soon.'
'She'd eat you up and spit you out in little bits and still be asking for more.'
'No she wouldn't.'
Bob butts in, looking at Bruce. 'You're too late mate; she's got her eye on lover boy here.'
'You lucky sod.' says Smoothy.
Lee has now finished his usual enormous breakfast, burps and joins in the conversation saying, 'I don't know, if I was a woman I'd sleep with him.'
The others cheer and throw plastic cups at Lee.

Present time

It's 1am and Mac decides to call it a day. He goes to the sink and washes the paint off his hands before crashing out on the bed and falling asleep.

The next day it's sunny and warm and Mac is in a pair of shorts and a T-shirt and is washing the Winnebago. Two boys appear on mountain bikes.
One of the boys says in a broad Devon accent, 'Do you want a hand mister?'
Mac slaps his stomach and answers, 'I need the exercise.'
The second boy says, 'Take you a week to wash that on your own.'
'A man like me, I'll do it in an hour.'
'Bet you can't,' says the first boy.
'Watch.'
The two boys get off their bikes and stand and watch.
Mac continues to wash the Winnebago but realises, he is taking on a mammoth task and begins to tire.
He stops and turns to the boys. 'How much?'
'A fiver each,' says the first boy.
Mac shakes his head and says, 'between you both.'
'Six quid between us.'
'Ok, deal.'
The two boys start washing the Winnebago. Mac lies back on the grass and sunbathes.
He makes a remark to the boys. 'You missed a bit.'
'No we aint.'
Mac points to the wheel. 'There, over by the wheel arch.'
The second boy washes the wheel arch and says, 'there's nothing there, it's the light.'
Mac gets up to look for himself, for a moment he stares as if in a dream. Then he says in a slow voice. 'There's nothing there, you're right, there's nothing there.'
The boys eventually finish washing the Winnebago and Mac pays them.
They get on their bikes and ride off shouting, 'Thanks mister. We always likes to help.'
Mac goes into the Winnebago. When he comes back out he is dressed in leather and is carrying a motorcycle helmet. He goes to the back of the Winnebago where a motorcycle is chained to a rack and takes the motorcycle off. After checking it over he starts it up and rides off towards Torquay.

In a small supermarket in Torquay Mac is busy shopping when he meets Alex, who is also shopping. Mac seems pre-occupied and a little frosty towards Alex.
Alex makes light conversation and says, 'I see the Martians haven't taken you away then?'

'I wish they would sometimes.'
Alex tries to snap Mac out of his mood. 'There's a night dive on later.'
'Another time Alex, but thanks.' Mac reaches for a loaf of bread.
'I wouldn't bother with that crap, there's a decent bakery next door.'
Mac still seems pre-occupied and puts the bread in his basket and continues with his shopping.
They bump into each other again.
'Sorry Alex, I had a bad night last night. Where do you get the bread from?'
'Next door.'
'And what time is the dive?'
'Be at the shop for seven thirty.'
Mac breaks a smile. 'Ok count me in.'

It's dusk and the dive boat is heading out to sea.
Mac is holding his DV looking thoughtfully, Alex notices.
'Problems?'
'No'
Mac pauses for a while, still looking at his DV. 'If this was working on the surface but not in the water, what would you do?'
'Panic.'
Mac replies, in a calm voice and says, 'But I didn't.'
Alex looks at Mac wondering what he is on about.
Mac continues. 'What would you say was wrong with it, working on the surface but not in the water?'
'This one, or hypothetically?'
'Hypothetically.'
'I'd say water was affecting the air flow valves.'
'At six feet?'
Alex replies, sounding a little unsure. 'Erm.... I'd check the air adjustment on the second stage.'
'It was done and checked.'
The coxswain of the boat, Geoff Lee interrupts. 'Nearly there Alex.'
Alex shouts back, 'OK,' and begins to attach the first stage of his breathing valve to the air tank.
As he is doing so he shouts to Mac. 'The air hose must have been blocked!'
Mac says nothing, just watches Alex putting his gear together.
Alex looks over towards Mac, waiting for an answer. There is no answer, so he continues, 'Are you sure the air hose wasn't blocked?'

Mac has the first stage of his valve in his hand and says, 'If you reduce the first stage pressure it would work on the surface but not in the water wouldn't it?'
'But you'd also need a screwdriver and a lot of effort to give yourself a problem, why bother?'
Mac doesn't answer but begins to attach his diving valve to his air tank.
Mac, Alex and some other divers enter the water and start their night dive.

Chapter 9

Return to London

Present time

It is night time, and Mac is in his Winnebago. The radio is on and Mac is working on a painting of the diving team. Bob's face is becoming more prominent in the painting.
As he paints his mind drifts back to the past….

Flashback

Mac arrives at the Police Station. As he locks his car, he sees Bob come out of the back entrance of the Police Station and run to a waiting parked car. The car takes off at speed; Mac continues into the police station and climbs the stairs to the diving unit headquarters. As he passes the equipment room, he sees a small orange-handled dumpy screwdriver on the floor.
Without a thought, he picks it up and puts it back on the shelf.

Present time

Mac comes out of his thoughts from the past and is staring at the finished painting of the dive team and particularly Bob.
He picks up his mobile phone and makes a call. 'Alex, it's Mac, did I wake you? Sorry I thought you might be up.'
Mac looks at his watch and is surprised to see it's four thirty in the morning, but continues, 'Look I need a favour.'

Next day Mac and Alex are looking around a beaten up old Transit Van. Mac looks unsure, scratching his chin and says to Alex,
'Are you sure this is legal?'
'It's passed its MOT.'
Mac laughs. 'Which year?'
Mac gets into the driver's seat and tries to close the door, it takes a couple of slams to secure the door. He adjusts the side mirror, and it comes off in his hand.
Alex jumps into the passenger seat and starts fiddling with the radio. He tunes into a local pop station and says, 'The radio works.'

‘Never mind the radio, where’s the key to this heap of junk?’
Alex smiles and hands him a screwdriver.
‘You got to be joking.’
Mac places the screwdriver into the ignition key slot, turns it and to his surprise the engine burst into life.
Alex trying to be serious says to Mac, ‘Remember when you park it on a hill leave it in first gear.’
Mac turns to Alex with a worried look on his face. ‘Are you sure it’s ok?’
‘Nothing to worry about, the body’s a bit shoddy, but she runs as sweet as a nut.’

Some hours later Mac is driving into central London. As he passes over Tower Bridge, he glances at the river Thames. The river traffic and the police boat passing under the bridge remind him of better times gone by, and how good life was when he was patrolling up and down the River Thames.
Mac drives on through the city and into London Docklands and pulls up along the side of Albert dock, looking across towards City Airport. He begins to feel cold, and shivers as he remembers the last time he was there.

Flashback

Bruce gives the ‘ok’ signal to his lifeline handler but then sees Mac looking at him and gives him a wanker sign with his hand.
Bruce then descends into the water and the jetty explodes.

Present time

Mac suddenly realizes he is daydreaming. He drives off and eventually finds a cheap bed and breakfast to stay in.
He arranges to meet his brother Forbes in a pub on the Isle of Dogs called The Gun, near the West India Dock entrance. Mac and Forbes spent many a good time in The Gun, and the landlord was the first to put Mac’s paintings on the wall and sell one. After that, there was no stopping Mac and his paintbrush, besides it was a good excuse to make regular visits to the pub.

As he stands alone in the back bar that overlooks the river Thames he remembers the lovely times he spent at Blackwall Thames Police

Station as a boat handler, years before he was accepted for the diving unit. Back then life seemed simple, get in the boat, patrol up the river at a leisurely speed with two other officers, checking out all the ships from different places in the world and when you finished a couple of pints in the Gun Public House. Even that was not forever; Blackwall Police station was later closed and then sold, to be turned into Luxury apartments. The paintings that Les, the landlord, used to let Mac put on the pub walls are now gone, along with Les and his family.

Having downed two pints of beer in half an hour Forbes eventually appears in the pub doorway. 'Given up the ghost already?'
Mac turns from the bar and smiles. 'Hi, big brother, what you drinking?'
'I'll get them in; you go and sit by the table in the corner.'
Mac goes over to the table, but stands looking at the new pictures on the wall, of the docks before they closed down. Forbes comes over with two pints of beer and they both sit down.
Forbes cannot help coming out with a negative comment. 'You can't hack this nomadic lifestyle can you, and you're back for a bit of London's fumes, queues, and hassle? I knew you wouldn't stick it.'
Mac replies with conviction. 'Wrong.'
'Go on then surprise me.'
Mac leans forward and says, 'What if someone in the dive team tampered with my diving equipment?'
Forbes looks at him as if he is mad. 'You've driven all this way to tell me that?'
'Yes I guess I have.'
Forbes replies, now sounding a little angry, 'Well you should have stopped off at the Hospital first and saved me the bother of telling you you're sodding mad.'
Mac gets up and says, 'Ok I'll see you later.'
Forbes grabs his arm. 'Sit down and finish your pint.'

The two brothers sit looking at each other and drinking.
Mac breaks the silence. 'The explosives must have been planted weeks ahead, probably hidden with the best camouflage job of the century.'
Forbes takes a large gulp of his beer. 'Which you missed.'
'Ok, maybe everyone was right, I missed it because I was preoccupied with trying to stay alive. My breathing equipment was not giving me air.'
'But?'

'But, with or without a hangover, a diver of my experience does not panic and beat his air valve in eight feet of water.'
Forbes takes a long look at his brother, takes another large gulp of beer and says, 'So you tell me, why would someone from the dive team want to blow up Carlos Azeglio?'
'They probably didn't. Maybe they were giving someone else a helping hand!'

Forbes and Mac spend the whole evening together drinking. When it's time to leave the pub he asks Mac, 'So where are you staying while you're here?'
'A small bed and breakfast in south London.'
'I'm not having that. You can stay at my luxury apartment in North London.'

Forbes lives in a small garden Flat in Islington. They approach Forbes's apartment front door. They look at each other then burst out laughing. Suddenly, Forbes turns serious and says, 'Who do you think did it?'
Mac replies, with some conviction. 'Bob.'
'Is that why you've come back?'
'I want to let it go and get on with my life, but it won't let me.'

The next morning Mac wakes up on the sofa. He has a splitting headache from all the drinking the night before. Forbes comes into the room, looking very rough; he is hung over but ready and dressed for work.
He hands Mac a glass of fizzing Andrew's liver salts saying, 'Here take this, it might help.'
Mac takes the glass and takes a sip. 'Cheers bruv that will do for breakfast.'
'Why are you pointing the finger at Bob?'
Mac does not want to answer the question yet but replies, 'He was late at the station on Wednesday night.'
Forbes says sarcastically, 'He was late at the station; well we should definitely hang the sod shouldn't we?'
Mac replies angrily, "Me going off the rails gave them a nicely wrapped package. Nobody asks any questions and the headlines read, 'beer swilling copper misses bomb', end of the story."
Not wanting to continue the conversation now that Mac is angry, Forbes says, 'Look I'm late for work I must go. We'll talk about this later.'
He throws Mac a spare set of house keys and leaves.

Sometime later Mac is parked in the transit van outside a house in south London; he is drawing on a piece of paper. As he is drawing, he hears a front door close. He looks up from his drawing and sees someone cross the road and get into a car. It is Bob.
Bob drives off and Mac follows in his transit van.

After a while Bob pulls up outside a lockup in the back streets of Kings Cross. Mac maintains a reasonable distance, so that he is not noticed. He can see Bob talking to a dark-haired man with a Mediterranean appearance. They begin to transfer small boxes from the man's Mercedes to Bob's car. The man then parks his car in front of the lock up and gets into Bob's car, and they drive off.
Mac records the registration of the Mercedes and then follows Bob's car. They pull up outside a bank, and both go in. A while later they return to the car and drive off, with Mac following.

The man in the car with Bob is George, 33 years old, his features very similar to Bob, although he is of Mediterranean appearance and speaks with a London accent.
Bob turns to George. 'Is that bastard still there?'
George looks over his shoulder. 'Yes. How long has he been following you?'
Bob replies, 'I'm not sure.'
Mac sees George look back and realises they may have seen he is following them so he pulls off at the next turning.

It is night, and for a change, Mac and Forbes are drinking tea in Forbes's kitchen.
Forbes says, 'I did a bit of checking today and looked at Bob's file. He's coming out of the police force.'
'When?'
'In a couple of months, if what I read is correct.'
'That's a big surprise. I thought he'd be a lifer like you.'
'I wonder what he's going to do.'
'Rumour is he's going to buy a wine bar in Bermondsey, or so I've heard through the grapevine.'
He continues, 'Oops, sorry about the pun.'
'On a copper's salary?'
'Doesn't make him guilty Mac.'
'Convenient though, wouldn't you say?'
'It doesn't mean anything.'

Mac has found out where Bob's new wine bar is and is sitting across the road from it in his transit van. There is a refit in progress. Bob arrives in his car and enters the bar. George is already inside.
'What do you think?' says George.
He flicks a switch and all the lights come on.
Bob looks at the lighting and smiles. 'That's great but we are going to need more lights in that corner, it's too dark.'
'I see he's still out there?'
'Been there since nine o'clock this morning.' says George.
They both walk to the window, which has one-way glass. They can see out but Mac cannot see into the bar.
'So what does he want?'
'I'm not sure, but I have a pretty good idea.' Bob replies.

In an office in a Police station, Forbes is working at his desk when a PC approaches and says, 'What you done this time Forbes?'
'Nothing, Why?'
'You've been summoned by the great lord and master himself.'
'You are joking, I hope.'
'Do I look like a jester?'
'That's for me to know and for you to wonder.' replies Forbes with a smile on his face.
'Honest he wants to see you.'
With no hurry Forbes puts his pen down, gets up from his desk, and follows the PC to Chief Superintendent Brian Samways' office.
The PC opens the door for Forbes, and he walks up to Brian's desk.
In an angry voice Brian says, 'What the bloody hell is your brother doing snooping around London like a private detective, Mackenzie?'
Forbes is shocked that his brother has been found out and that it has got back to Brian.
Forbes, thinking fast, decided to be direct rather than bullshit Brian.
'He feels sir, that there are still some unanswered questions and cannot seem to rest until he has them answered.'
Brian calms down and speaks in a softer voice. 'Well the Metropolitan Police Force feels that all the questions have been answered. Is there something we have overlooked then?'
'Not to my knowledge sir.'
'Three good officers lost their lives and one lost his job, pension and marriage. It would be a shame if we had a fifth casualty, wouldn't you agree?' says Brian looking Forbes straight in the eye.
'Yes sir.'

'It's was your brother's mistake, let's not make it yours as well, and the case is closed as far as I am concerned.'
The phone rings and Brian picks it up and continues, 'You can go now Mackenzie, good day.'

In the diving equipment and service room, Bob is cleaning a diving valve when Tony enters with two cups of tea.
'Thanks Tony, when does the new boy arrive?'
A PC walks by and looks into the equipment and service room.
Tony waits for him to pass. Bob notices this, and as Tony's attention comes back to him, he carries on cleaning the DV.
'William Mackenzie has been asking questions about the explosion, and you in particular, is there something we should know Bob?'
'Like what?' Replies Bob still occupied with the servicing the DV.
'I don't know, you tell me.'
Bob put the valve down, and turns to look at Tony in the eye and says in a forceful voice. 'Look, I have no idea why he is asking questions. He's a certified nutter isn't he?'
'This has nothing to do with you leaving has it?'
Bob looking defensive says, 'I am leaving because I've had enough of the force, and I want out, that's all there is to say. Now if you don't mind I have work to do.'
Bob continues with his work on the diving valve but Tony feels unsure with Bob's answers.

In Forbes' kitchen, Mac is on the telephone. 'Alex, I need to stay in London for a few more days ......good man, can you check on the Winnebago for me? Yes a Winnebago, its home and I'm feeling homesick, and you'll be pleased to know I got the handbrake fixed on the van.'
As Mac hangs up the telephone, Forbes enters the flat and slams the door. He is in a very bad mood, and Mac knows it.
'Hi'
Forbes ignores Mac, and goes straight to the fridge and takes out a beer. 'I got my legs slapped today, and they know you are here.'
'Am I not allowed to stay with my brother?'
Forbes takes a large gulp of beer from his can and looks at Mac straight in the eye saying, 'What was it that nurse said to you at the nut house? Oh yes I remember; what is right for one person isn't necessarily good for another. Well she's right, because I'm not going to spend the next twenty years living in a caravan. It's over Mac, you missed it, and you've just got to learn to live with it.'

Mac replies sounding apologetic. 'Forbes I'm sorry to involve you, but it's not over, I'll move out tomorrow.'
'You are going to stay in London then?'
'Yes for a few more days.'
'Where?' Asks Forbes now in a calmer voice.
'I'll find somewhere.' Says Mac, sounding a little concerned.
'Mac you can stay here as long as you like, I wouldn't hear of anything else, but I trust you as a brother not to jeopardise my future in the Force.'

The following day Mac is sitting in his van parked away from the wine bar. He thinks he is being discrete. Bob's car is in view, parked outside the wine bar. All of a sudden, as if by magic, Bob appears from nowhere with two cups of tea. He makes Mac jump as he comes up alongside the open driver's window and with a smile says, 'Two sugars as I remember.'
He hands Mac a cup of tea, which he takes. 'It's one actually but two's fine, thanks.'
'So what's going on?' asks Bob with a false smile on his face.
Mac takes a sip of his tea. 'I don't know I was hoping you could tell me?'
'Well why don't you come and have a look, you won't see much from here.'
In the wine bar, there are a couple of men working. George is supervising the refit. Mac and Bob enter the wine bar, still with the cups of tea in their hands.
'What do you think then?'
'How are you paying for it on a Policeman's pay?'
'I can see why you didn't make the diplomatic corps. Hopefully this is my future. It's all legal so get off my back Mac; I know it's not the first time you've been snooping around here.'
Being blunt again and looking at George Mac asks, 'Who's your friend?'
There is no smile on Bob's face now, as he replies, 'No, your turn, why are you following me?'
Mac looks at Bob straight in the eye, entering his personal space and says, 'Because there are a few things that don't add up on the day of the explosion.'
Bob is now getting very wound up and angrily replies, 'Get a bloody calculator then.'
Mac stays calm and says, 'If it would solve it for me, I would, but unfortunately I need to ask you!'
Bob now trying to sound unconcerned replies, 'Ask away.'

'Why would two DV's that have regular checks both have the same mysterious problem on the same day?'
'I have no idea. Now you've had your question so just piss off and get on with your life, and I'll get on with mine.'

Mac is infuriated with his dismissal of the questions and lunges at Bob wrestling him to the floor. George and the two workmen rush over and pull Mac and Bob apart.
Bob wipes blood off his mouth and says, 'Leave him, he's not worth it.'
The two workmen let go of Mac, and he adjusts his clothing and leaves the bar.
George closes the door behind Mac and turns to Bob. 'What was that all about?'
Still wiping blood from his mouth Bob replies, 'Some people just can't handle the truth, they should never have let him out of the nut house.'

Back at work the next day in the divers' mess room, Bob, Smoothy and John are assembling for the start of the day. They sit around waiting for other members of the team to arrive. Bob has a newspaper in front of him, but is staring intently at a photograph pinned to the mess wall. The photo is of Chris being kissed by a male stripper. The full dive team is also shown in the photo, with the exception of Bruce.

John turns to Smoothy who is busy demolishing a large ham roll and asks, 'Where are we diving tomorrow Smoothy?'
'I think we are at the reservoir.' replies Smoothy, and then asks,
'Anyone want a drink?'
As he goes to the kitchen to make some tea, Bob says, 'Oh no thanks.'
'What's on the telly tonight Bob?'
Bob hands him the newspaper saying, 'Here look for yourself.' and continues, 'I will have a tea Smoothy.'
Bob then gets up from his chair and walks out of the door saying, 'Back in a minute.'
As Bob walks along the corridor looking at the dive team notice board, he sees Sergeant Tony Hayes exit his office, walk along the corridor and enter another room.
Bob walks into Tony's office, unfastens the latch to the window, then walks out and double steps further along the corridor and into the toilet. Tony meanwhile comes out of the other room and enters his office, closing the door behind him.

The dive team has returned to the Police Station after a routine day diving, they were looking for a safe in the river and checking out a car that had been driven into the London Docks. They have all assembled in the mess room for a debrief.
Smoothy, John and Bob are present when Sergeant Tony Hays enters the mess room.
'Everyone ok?' he enquires. 'No aches and pains? Right, if all goes to plan, and we don't get a call out in the middle of the night, tomorrow we'll be looking for a shotgun used in a raid on the Nat West bank in Welling.'
'Smoothy and Ian?' Tony pauses. 'Where is Ian?'
'He was here a minute ago,' says Smoothy then continues, 'but you know what the new guys are like, probably polishing his DV or neck ring.'
'Okay Smoothy you can fill him in when he returns. Smoothy, you and Ian will be in the water, John, Bob and I will be on the surface.' Tony continues, 'I'm expecting this to be a quick and easy one. The CID are bringing someone down to point to the spot.'
'What time do you want us here?' asks John.
'Hopefully we should be finished by one. Make sure Ian is not late, will you?'
Tony walks out of the mess room and then back down the corridor to his office. He checks the door is locked and then leaves the Unit Flat. Bob has been watching him and then leaves himself.

It is about ten at night. Bob enters the Police Station, carrying a sports bag. There is a squash racket sticking out of the side.
As he goes up the stairs, he meets Sam, the station cleaner. Sam is a very reliable and honest man, but appears to be slightly retarded, apart from when you engage him in conversation about Ireland and the IRA. He then knows no bounds, and will give you a very detailed history lesson on Ireland and the troubles.
Bob smiles at him saying, 'Hi Sam.'
Sam stops mopping, looks at Bob with open staring eyes that would frighten anyone who did not know him. 'I've cleaned up there.' he replies.
Bob turns back and smiles again. 'Don't worry Sam, I'll leave it as I find it, promise.'

Bob continues up the stairway to the flat that is the dive team's headquarters. He looks in a couple of rooms to make sure no one is there and continues along the corridor. He walks past Tony's office

and turns the door handle only to find that it's locked. He continues on to the shower room next to the office, and locks the door behind him. Bob turns the shower on and opens his sports bag and takes out a small rucksack, which he puts over his shoulders. He walks to the window, opens it and looks down at the street three floors below.

The street is deserted; no one is about. He then climbs out of the window and steps onto a narrow ledge and slowly makes his way to Tony's office. He startles a dozing pigeon, which flies into his face, and for what seems an eternity he has a face full of feathers and almost loses his footing. He stops for a moment, his heart is beating so fast he can feel it pounding in his ears, and he is sweating with fear. He remembers his training and how to keep calm in a stressful situation, breathing in and out slowly until his heart beat returns to normal. Bob then continues along the ledge until he reaches the window of Tony's office.

His thought is that the only thing that can go wrong now is the window being locked. To his relief, it is still unlatched, and he climbs in. Once inside the office Bob walks over to the filing cabinet.
He opens the top drawer and pulls out a large file, which is marked in capitals DIVE ROSTERS. He opens the file to reveal all the dive rosters for the last two years. He works his way through the roster to a particular section and removes about a dozen pages, and then opens his rucksack and takes out a large black cloth sheet that will hide the light from the photocopy machine.

Bob walks over to the photocopy machine, and puts the pages he has taken from the file into the feed side of the photocopier. He then places the black sheet over the photocopier, presses the start button and sits down to wait. The machine starts churning out copies but the light that is normally thrown out by the copier cannot be seen.
When all the copying is finished Bob replaces the original dive logs into the file and puts it back into the filing cabinet. He then folds the copies of the dive logs and puts them into his rucksack.

Bob climbs out of the window onto the ledge again and begins his perilous walk back to the shower room, this time looking out for pigeons. However, on his return it's not pigeons he has to worry about. There is a drunk lying on the pavement, looking directly up at him. He stops dead as the drunk shouts, in a loud slurred voice. 'What you doing up there?'

Suddenly, two police officers arrive and put the drunk up on his feet. The drunk slurs. 'Hey, there's a man on the roof.'
Fortunately, for Bob they don't look up, and say to the drunk, 'Come on now we'll take you for a nice lie down.'
They then disappear with the drunk into the Police Station.

Bob continues on and climbs into the shower room, closes the window behind him, turns the shower off and places the rucksack into the sports bag. He unlocks the door and is about to leave, but returns and wets his hair.
As he walks down the stairs, Sam is still cleaning.
'Left it as I found it Sam.'
'I hope so.' says Sam.
'Goodnight.' Says Bob and leaves the Police Station.

It's late at night; Mac is alone in his brother's lounge, drawing what appears to be a jetty at City Airport. There is a knock at the door. When he opens it, he is surprised to see Bob standing there.
Bob is wearing a pair of gloves and holding a large brown envelope.
'I've got something for you!'
He hands Mac the envelope.
Mac looks at it curiously, and then looks at Bob. 'Is it a bomb?'
'They're the dive rosters for the six weeks coming up to the City Airport search.'
'And why would I want these?' asks Mac suspiciously.
'Have a look and see what you think.'
Bob turns to leave then swings back saying, 'If you find anything interesting let me know.'
Bob gets into his car and drives away into the night.

The following night Mac is again alone in Forbes' kitchen. He is sitting at a table scanning the dive rosters, and making many notes.
He hears a key in the front door, and scrambles to hide the dive rosters, and the notes he has made. He manages to get them hidden in a cupboard before Forbes enters. Mac tries to look relaxed as Forbes enters the kitchen.
With a sigh Forbes says, 'Hi, what a day. So what have you been doing?'
'This and that.'
Forbes thinks that is a very non-committal answer and is immediately suspicious.
'You look suspicious.'
'You've been a copper for too long.'

'I'm tired that's all.'
'That makes two of us bruv.' says Forbes, 'I'm off to bed, goodnight.'
'Goodnight Forbes, pleasant dreams.'
As Forbes goes to his bedroom, he shouts. 'Turn the light off will you.'
Mac retrieves the rosters and his notes from the cupboard and shouts. 'Will do, won't be long behind you.'

Mac works through the dive rosters and begins to see a pattern. It is now very early in the morning, and Mac has fallen asleep while working. Forbes enters the kitchen, having seen the light on when he got up to use the toilet. He sees Mac with his head on the table and the roster sheets in front of him. Forbes picks up a few pages and realizes what they are, then puts them down and turns the light off, which wakes Mac up. He puts the light back on when he realizes Mac is awake and picks up the roster sheets, waving them in the air saying, 'Where did you get these?'
Mac replies, rubbing his eyes, 'Bob.'
Forbes says angrily, 'I don't know if I should smack you in the mouth or throw you out.'
Mac tries to reason with him. 'Listen to me first Forbes and then you can smack me in the mouth.'
Forbes sits down the other side of the table and folds his arms. 'You've got 30 seconds.'

Mac starts his explanation. 'The unit dives by roster, that way no one can choose a dive. You have to take the rough with the smooth. The name at the top of the roster dives that day, and once you have completed the dive you go to the bottom of the roster until your name works its way up to the top again.'
Forbes, sounding sarcastic, replies, 'That was interesting.'
Mac ignores his sarcasms and continues. 'If someone's ill, has a day off, the name at the top will change the sequence.'
Forbes still with arms folded starts to count aloud. 'Ten, nine, eight ……….'
Mac just continues, 'The point is, the roster is always changing, it never keeps to a set plan. Don't you see this applies to City Airport? Say I'd been ill the week before. Instead of being in C section, I would have dived in A section.'
Forbes is still counting. 'Five, four……..'
Unperturbed Mac continues, 'Bruce always worked at it, so I would be in C and D section.'
Forbes stops counting and gets curious. 'Go on.'

Mac picks up one of the roster sheets and shows it to Forbes. 'Look at this. Lee cut himself on one of the jobs, so he has two days off. If Lee hadn't had the two days off, the roster would have stayed the same from the day he dived, and that would have meant at the City Airport search I would have dived in F section with Bruce.'
Mac continues now knowing he has Forbes' full attention. 'Two day later who has a day off?'
'Bruce.' says Forbes.
'Yes, putting me back in section C.'
Mac now pleased he has Forbes' interest again says, 'Every time. How am I doing?'
Forbes smiles. 'You've still got your teeth haven't you?'

On an embankment of the River Thames in Bermondsey, Bob is leaning on the railings looking towards Tower Bridge.
Mac approaches him from behind and says, 'Talk to me.'
Bob turns around and puts his finger to his lips, indicating silence.
He then proceeds to search Mac, frisking him up and down.
'What's going on Bob, I'm on your side mate?'
'I wouldn't want you recording our conversation for posterity, can't be too careful these days.'

With Bob now satisfied, they walk along the embankment, and Bob says, 'I did most of my dive training at City Airport docks, and Bruce was always asking me questions about it, then one day out of the blue I realised, he was manipulating the roster.'
'Why didn't you say anything to anyone?'
Bob stops walking and turns to face Mac. 'Look I told you once, I don't know. As far I am I concerned, we are nothing but cannon fodder. They know if there is a bomb planted anywhere we search, chances are we will be the ones to cop it. That's why I'm coming out the Force, because it will happen again.'
Mac says suspiciously, 'For all I know you could have altered these rosters.'
'Yes I could have, but who asked Bruce to dive in our section, I didn't, did you?'
'Tony did.' replies Mac.
'He didn't. Bruce volunteered out of the blue for reasons only known to himself.' Bob holds out his hand to Mac. 'Give me those, I'll show you something else, you ungrateful bastard.'
Mac hands Bob the envelope containing the dive rosters. To his complete surprise Bob throws them into the River Thames. There is a

moment of silence as both watch the strong current take them downriver, and disappear under the bows of a passing pleasure boat. 'It's the best place for them.' says Bob, and continues, 'I don't like all this attention, it might scare someone into doing something that I'll be on the receiving end of, and if I see you again I'll deal with it personally.'
Mac, annoyed at losing the copy rosters turns to Bob and says, 'You're a gutless tosser.'
'You might be right there, but I'm alive and I intend to stay that way.'
Bob and Mac walk away from each other in opposite directions without so much as a goodbye.

Mac decides to walk to St James Park, where he used to search the lake prior to the Trooping the Colour. He always found it peaceful there, an oasis in the middle of the hustle and bustle of London.
After the early morning search, the unit had to remain on station, in case the bridge the soldiers used to get back to the barracks on dispersing after the Trooping the Colour, did blow up.
One of his two daughters, Lisa, who worked at the Treasury only a stone's throw away, always took the opportunity to meet her dad for lunch in the park and catch up with what was going on in his life.

He finds a park bench near the bridge they used to search, and remembers that fortunately they never ever found any explosives, just amusing things like umbrellas, spectacles, cameras and coins. Mac relaxes and watches a couple walking hand in hand with their dog trailing behind on a long lead.
He starts daydreaming and enters a flashback in his mind.

Flashback

He is looking out of the police station window into the forecourt.
He sees Bruce walking towards the station, carrying a box of files.
As Bruce walks past a dog van parked in the forecourt, the police dog, a police sniffer dog used for finding explosives, jumps up at the van window and barks loudly. This makes Bruce drop the box of files.
The incident causes other police officers in the forecourt to laugh at Bruce, but he takes it in good humour and bows to them. Several officers come to his assistance and help him pick up the files.

Present Time

'Hello, what are you doing here?' says a voice that brings Mac out of his daydream.

He looks up and sees Forbes holding a packet of sandwiches.

'Oh, just needed some peace and quiet, and I've always liked St James Park It has some pleasant memories.'

'Me too, I always come here when I get the opportunity, mind if I join you on the bench, Mac?'

'No take a pew bruv.'

Forbes sits next to his brother and takes a bite out of one of the sandwiches saying, as he is chewing, 'How's Bob?'

'A defender of the Crown he is not.'

'So why you and not somebody else?'

'Chris used to say Mac dives with a Zimmer frame, and being the oldest in the team, they would take bets as to whether I would pass the next medical.'

Taking another bite of his sandwich, Forbes replies, 'And suddenly the joke becomes a problem.'

'But they didn't have to bother did they?'

'I need another favour, Forbes.'

'That depends.'

'I'm being watched. It's like being back at school.'

'Except this time you got sent home and you had to stay, yes?'

Mac does not reply so Forbes continues. 'Bruce was in the process of getting a divorce. Her name was Lorraine, where is she now and what is she doing?'

'I've no idea.'

Forbes gets up to leave and offers the last sandwich to Mac.

'No thanks, I'm not hungry.'

'Ok. I'll see what I can find out.'

As Forbes walks away, Mac shouts, 'Blood is thicker than water.'

Forbes turns and shouts back, 'That's the one.'

Chapter 10

Key to the door

In a police dog compound, Ray Dohoo, 44, an experienced police dog handler, has his back to the main entrance of the compound and hears a voice he recognises.
'Hello Ugly.'
Without turning, he says, 'The dulcet tones of Mr. Mackenzie.'
Ray turns around and smiles. 'Long time no see. How are things with you Mac?'
'Oh ducking and diving.'
'Not so much of the diving now so I hear. Heard you'd become a new age traveller now.'
'Who told you that, Ray?'
'News travels fast in the Force, some nasty, bad politics over that City Airport explosion.'
Mac bends down, stroking one of the dogs in the compound, and says, 'It makes you philosophical.'
'Swallowed a dictionary, have you?' Replies Ray with a smile.
Stroking the dog again, Mac asks, 'What's her name?'
'Bridgett. Named after my first girlfriend.'
'She's a gorgeous dog.'
'She was a gorgeous girlfriend.'
Mac gets to the point of his visit and asks Ray, 'If I'd been handling explosives would she bark now?'
'Depends.'
'Depends on what, Ray?'
Ray starts to explain with the extensive knowledge he has gained over the years working with police sniffer dogs. 'Some explosives, God help us, don't smell, but Semtex, which is a commonly used explosive, mainly because it can be moulded like plasticine into any shape, smells like marzipan.'
'So if you'd handled Semtex or just made a Christmas cake she'd go barking mad.'
Mac thanks Ray for his help and leaves the dog compound and heads back to his brother's flat. In the kitchen, Mac sees a folded piece of paper with his name on it.
He unfolds the paper and reads the note, smiles, and leaves the flat.

On the outskirts of London in a down-market housing estate, there are some children playing in the street. Mac has a piece of paper in his hand. He is looking at an address written on the paper and trying to match it with one of the houses on the estate, but most have their numbers missing. Nearby he can see a woman putting rubbish into a dustbin. Her name is Lorraine Rembridge and she is 29 years old.
There is a gentle and friendly look about her, slightly overweight with a round smooth face.

Lorraine spots Mac looking at the piece of paper and peering at the houses around him. Lorraine recognises him and shouts, 'A rough guess, I'd say it's me you are looking for?'
Mac turns and smiles at Lorraine. 'Hello Lorraine, yes I am.'
Lorraine invites Mac into her house and asks him to take a seat in the lounge. Kids can be heard upstairs being very noisy, and Lorraine can see Mac looking in the direction of the noise.
'They can drive you mad sometimes.'
Lorraine walks to the foot of the stairs.
'What are you doing you two?'
The noise continues.
'Hang on a minute.'

Lorraine climbs the stairs and Mac begins to look around the lounge. On top of the television is a picture of Bruce, Lorraine and a young boy. They are posing by a new Ford Car. Lorraine returns to see Mac looking at the photo.
Mac says, 'He looks like his dad.'
'Moans like his dad too, I sometimes think he loved that car more than me.'
'I'm sorry to pry Lorraine.'
No, no you're not. When was the last time I saw you Mac?'
Not sure, eighteen months, two years ago.'
Being direct Lorraine asks Mac, 'So what do you want Mac, It's not a social call is it?'
'Some things about Bruce and the day of the explosion don't fit together, and I can't rest until the pieces fit together.'
Lorraine replies with a condescending voice, 'Looking to blame the dead are you?'
'No Lorraine, I'm looking for the truth.'
'Well you can blame the dead for all I care.'
The children upstairs start to make a noise again.
Lorraine walks to the bottom of the stairs and shouts, 'James you can go home and Ben you can go to bed if you don't be quiet.'

The noise stops and Mac continues. 'Before the explosion did Bruce acquire any new friends?'
Lorraine frowns and replies, 'Only that slag at the police station. None apart from her. He always had some new idea or scheme on the go, Richard Branson no, the nice boy from Dagenham with a wife and kid, yes, but the stupid idiot couldn't face it.'
'Is that why you didn't come to the funeral?'
'I wanted to scare him into what he might lose, but it didn't work. I'm sorry he's dead but he left me a long-time ago.'
One of the children starts to cry, but Lorraine continues, 'He stayed with his sister for the last year. Any deals he was up to would have gone there.'
The crying becomes louder. Lorraine angrily shouts, 'KIDS' and climbs the stairs.
Mac can hear her voice upstairs. 'I've warned you two.........'
Mac takes a last look around the lounge and leaves without saying goodbye.

In a new housing estate in Chislehurst, Mac approaches one of the houses and rings the front door bell. Gaynor Evans answers. 'Mac, I can't believe it, I thought you'd gone, er...'
Mac interrupts. 'Gone Mad?'
Gaynor smiles. 'Well if you have, you look good on it, come in.'
Mac steps into the hallway and Gaynor continues, 'Someone told me you were living in a tent?'
'It's a tent with wheels.' jokes Mac.
Mac can hear there is someone else in the house and a man's voice shouts from upstairs. 'Who's that?'
'It's William Mackenzie.'
The man shouts back. 'Who?'
Gaynor replies, 'Someone from work.'
She turns to Mac and asks, 'Would you like a cup of tea or something stronger maybe?'
'Tea would be lovely.'
They walk into the kitchen, and Mac sits down on a stool while Gaynor starts to make the tea. 'I need to talk to you about Bruce.'
Gaynor turns and looks at Mac frowning, then walks to the foot of the stairs and shouts, 'We've run out of milk, I'm going to pop down to the shop.'
The man shouts back. 'What?'
Gaynor repeats what she said in a louder voice. She then turns to Mac and in a whisper says, 'I can't talk here Mac.'

Then shouts to the man upstairs, 'Back in five minutes dear.'

Gaynor and Mac leave the house and walk down the street towards the shop.
'He was a handsome lad and good fun too.'
'Did you love him?'
Gaynor laughs. 'Worrying what he's doing every time your back is turned? No, you don't love people like Bruce.'
Gaynor stops walking and turns to face Mac. 'Oh God, Mac, you're not going to tell me he had some incurable disease are you?'
'I can't help you on that one Gaynor.'
'What do you want to know then?'
'How long did you go on seeing him for?'
'On and off about eight months I suppose.'
'Did he ever introduce you to anyone who was different? Not one of his usual circle of friends?'
Gaynor blushes. 'Um.. socializing wasn't top of our agenda if you know what I mean.'
Mac begins to write a telephone number on a piece of paper and hands it to Gaynor saying, 'If you think of anything Gaynor, please let me know?'
'Like what?'
'After he left his wife, he seems to have disappeared off the face of the planet for a while. I would be interested to know what he was doing then.'
Gaynor looks at the piece of paper with the phone number on it. 'Okay, I'll see what I can do, but don't hold your breath.'

It is night-time and Mac and Forbes are in a lift that services a council block of flats. The lift is made of grey metal and has graffiti everywhere. It smells as if someone has urinated inside the lift. Someone has written 'Gi'z a job' on the wall of the lift.
Forbes points to it and says, 'He can have mine if we get caught.'
The lift stops and the doors open. 'Thank God for that, any longer in there, and I would have been sick.'
Mac and Forbes step out onto the top floor of the tower block and have a splendid view of London at night through the corridor windows. Mac stops and takes in the London skyline. 'I used to think this was a great place, I'm not so sure now.'
Forbes is not listening and knocks on one of the flat doors.
Mac walks over to join him. A strong cockney voice can be heard the other side of the door saying, 'Who's that?'

Forbes shouts, Detective Forbes Mackenzie, I need to ask you a few questions about your brother.'
There is a long wait. A few doors down the corridor a door opens and a man looks out at Mac and Forbes. Then after what seems an eternity the door opens and standing there is Andrea Fraser, 27 years old. She has blond hair and is dressed slightly tarty, with a very short skirt, low cut blouse and thick makeup, hiding her otherwise clear skin.
'Ok Batman and Robin, let's see your badges.'
Forbes gets out his warrant card and shouts to the man down the corridor, 'It's all right you can close your door now mate.'
The man waves and closes his door. Andrea looks intently at Mac.
'It was you who had the punch up at the funeral wasn't it? Come in then, don't just stand there you two.'
Forbes looks at Mac and grins. 'What's it like to be famous?'
'Go on Forbes just get in.'
They enter Andrea's lounge, the interior is tasteless and over decorated. Andrea starts by saying, 'It's typical of Bruce to get himself blown up and him owing me a grand. That's why I haven't heard from that bitch of a wife of his since.'

Andrea leaves the lounge and returns with a small suitcase saying,
'If you see the snobby cow you can give her this and tell her a cheque will be fine.'
Mac indicates he wants to open the case. 'May I?'
'As long as you take it away I don't care what you do with it.'
Mac opens the case slowly and asks, 'Did he leave anything else?'
'He had some new place he was moving into, but I don't know where it was.'
Forbes asks, 'How long was he here for?'
'Six, seven months, but we were like passing ships in the night, and before you ask I don't know where he went or what he was up to.'
Mac looks through the case, which has clothes, shaving gear, and expensive aftershave. He picks out a shirt that has the label Armani on it.
Andrea continues, 'He thought he was a playboy, Mr. Dreamer, wasted his money and his time. He was a waste of space really.'
Mac comes across a set of dog tags in the case. On the chain is a key.
'Do you know what this is for Andrea?'
'No, but he did have a lockup on East Hill, the key for that is here.'
Andrea goes to a vase on the sideboard and tips out a padlock key.
'Don't ask me which lock up because I don't know.'
There is a silent pause; Mac and Forbes look at Andrea.

She continues, 'If it doesn't concern me, I'm not interested.'
Mac enquires 'Do you have a baby boy?'
'No, why?'
'Just curious, that's all.'

It's late at night and Mac and Forbes are near a row of lock up garages. Forbes has a torch and Mac has the padlock key. They are trying one lock after another to see which one fits the key.
Forbes says in a whisper, 'What was all that about? A baby boy?'
'Bruce didn't turn up at Chris's birthday do because he said he was babysitting for his sister's little boy.'
'He was probably seeing Gaynor.'
'Maybe.'

As they try the next lock Forbes whispers, 'I wonder if this comes under breaking and entering?'
'If you had a crow bar in your hand, I'd be more worried brother.'
Just then, the key Mac is trying turns in a lock. 'Bingo! Oops.' says Forbes in a loud voice, realising, he might attract attention.
'Yes Bingo' whispers Mac. 'Keep your voice down big mouth.'
They go in and Mac pulls the door down, closing it behind him before feeling for the light switch, and turns it on. To their disappointment, the lockup is bare, but he notices behind the light switch is jammed a postcard showing a small fishing village in Devon. Mac takes the postcard and looks at the back but it's blank. He replaces the card and Forbes says, 'Nothing, absolutely nothing. Where now?'
'What a surprise, not.'
'Come on Mac we've pushed our luck enough for one night, let's get out of here before we both get nicked.'

At a McDonalds restaurant Mac sits drawing on an empty hamburger bag with the logo McDonalds on it. He circles the letters C and D in the word. Forbes returns to the table with a tray of food and Mac looks up from what he is doing.
'Cheers Forbes, which one is mine?'
Forbes points to two containers on the tray. 'These two.'
Forbes watches someone put their rubbish in one of the large rubbish containers in the restaurant as he takes a big bite of his large burger.
'A pre-planted bomb causing that much damage would have to be in a container at least two feet by two feet, yes?'
'If not bigger.' replies Mac.

Forbes takes an even bigger bite of his hamburger and speaks with his mouth full. 'Even smashed out of your head you're not going to miss that, are you?'
Mac is pleased his brother is now beginning to see his side, and makes a cryptic remark. 'One convert at last, and just a few million to go.'
There is no stopping Forbes now, he seems more enthusiastic than ever and continues, 'If it was in the water planted away from the jetty then you'd always be looking the wrong way. Bruce chooses your dive and could have moved it to where you had already searched.'
Mac interjects 'Giving him the perfect alibi.'
'Except' Says Forbes, 'something goes wrong and boom.'
Mac takes a drink of coke and says, 'Great explanation Forbes, but based it's on no evidence, and is complicated by the small fact that our main suspect, who everyone seems to think is Mr Perfect, now happens to be a pile of ashes in a box,
'Except for his wife, who hates him.' says Forbes.
'And if you are right, why would he do it and for whom? Nobody ever claimed responsibility for the bomb, so we are back to square one.'
Forbes takes another large bite of his hamburger. 'This is great,' he mumbles through a mouth full of burger 'I'm sorry little brother but you're stuffed.'
Mac thinks 'So is your mouth big brother, every time you decide to speak.'
He smiles and says, 'Look Forbes, I've just got something I must do, you stay here and finish your burger, and I'll see you back at the flat.'
Forbes waves ok and carries on stuffing the burger into his mouth.

Mac travels back to the lock-up they were in the night before, and takes the postcard that is jammed behind the light switch.
He puts it into his pocket and leaves.

Chapter 11

Return to The Westcountry

The next day Mac drives back to the West Country and picks up his Winnebago motor caravan. He wastes no time in researching the postcard and drives to a small cove on the south coast of Devon that resembles the picture on the postcard. As he enters the village, he sees a sign saying, welcome to the village of Beer.

The cove is dotted with small fishermen's cottages and has a pub called 'The Anchor Inn'. There is no parking in the village, so he finds a large car park on the outskirts where he parks his Winnebago. After locking up the, he starts walking down the narrow streets to The Anchor Pub.

On entering the pub, he orders a pint of local beer. He notices a man alone at the end of the bar, whose glass is empty and asks the barman, 'what is the man at the end of the bar drinking?'
The barman pours another pint of local beer and hands it to the man, who says in a broad Devon accent 'Thanks mate, very kind of you.'
Mac walks over to join him and takes out a photo of Bruce.
'On holiday are you?'
'Yes, I'm looking for an old friend of mine. Have you seen him?'
Mac shows him the picture of Bruce. He looks at the photo, then at Mac and gives a sharp 'No, sorry I can't help you.'
Mac replies, 'Stupid question really.'
The barman who was also looking at the photo scowls, 'Yes' and walks away.
Mac calls the barman back and asks, 'Who's the best looking woman around here, barman?'
The man at the end of the bar laughs, 'That will be Laura.'
'Who's she?'
'She's the reason why every man around here has short hair.' replies the barman.
The barman and the man begin to laugh.
Then the man at the end of the bar says, 'She's a hairdresser.'
Mac finishes his pint and leaves the bar looking for the hairdresser's shop.

He finds it, walks in, and talks to a young woman behind a counter situated just inside the entrance to the shop. She points to a very attractive woman busy cutting a customer's hair. Mac takes the photo of Bruce out of his pocket as Laura stops cutting the customer's hair and walks over to Mac. She reacts to the photo, and gives Mac some information. He leaves the shop smiling.

At a deserted house on the south coast of Devon, not far from the cove, Mac is driving his Winnebago up a long drive that leads to a house. As he gets to the house, he stops, gets out and surveys the scene. He then walks up to the front door, rings the doorbell and waits for an answer. There is no answer, so he looks around to make sure no one is anywhere near the house. He looks around once more and takes the dog tag with the key attached out of his pocket, and tries it in the door lock. The door opens and he enters the house.

It is silent apart from the sound of the waves crashing on the rocks not far away. The house is bare but clean. Mac enters the lounge and surveys the scene. There is a large sofa, expensive television and sound system but no other furnishings. He climbs the stairs and enters the master bedroom. There is a very large double bed with a mirror about the same size attached to the ceiling above the bed.
In one corner is a clothes rack with a cover over it. Mac removes the cover to discover the rack is full of expensive designer men's clothes.
He starts looking through the clothes and discovers inside one of the jacket pockets, several postcards. He removes the postcards and can see they are all the same as the one he found in the lock-up.

As if by instinct he looks on the back of each postcard and on one a longitude and latitude reading is written. Mac replaces all but the postcard with the reading back in the jacket pocket and walks away with the card to the window overlooking the sea. He stares at the number on the postcard and then back at the sea. He continues exploring the house and eventually enters the garage through a door leading off the kitchen. Inside the garage is a Mercedes 190E car.
Mac writes the registration number down. As he looks through the car window, he sees the same orange handled dumpy screwdriver that he saw in the police station. He tries to open the car door, but suddenly the silence is broken by the scream of the car's alarm.
Mac walks back to the lounge and picks up the telephone and, to his surprise, finds it is working. He dials a number. The car alarm can still be heard from the garage.
'It's me, what are you doing tomorrow?'

'Good, bring your dive gear, and Alex, can you bring a GPS? Fantastic, see you tomorrow about ten in the village.'
Mac puts the phone down and redials a new number. 'Forbes? Yes I'm fine, I need another favour. Can you check a registration for me?'
'Oh come on bruv. It's no skin off your nose. Ok it's a Mercedes M50BFM, call me back on my mobile, and I'll tell you then, and whatever you do, don't call this number.'
Mac puts the phone down, dials the speaking clock to cover last number redial, and puts the phone down. He leaves the house as quickly as he can. The car alarm is still screaming away as he drives back down the drive.

Mac has returned to Beer and is leaving a shop with a pint of milk.
He stops by the kerb and looks left and right before crossing. A car at the end of the street appears and stops. The car's lights are on full beam and whoever is driving flashes the lights. He pauses for a moment then begins to walk towards the car. As he does so, the car reverses around the corner then takes off at speed in the opposite direction with tyres screeching. Mac looks around him. He is alone, with not a soul in sight.

That night in his Winnebago Mac lies in bed fully clothed and has a blanket wrapped around him. He stares out of the skylight into the night sky. The wind is whistling outside making him feel quite alone.
He gets up to check he has locked the door and then opens a cupboard, and takes out a large diving knife.

He returns to his original position on the bed but this time with the diving knife in his hand under the blanket. Mac wakes up in a cold sweat, suddenly to feel the cold steel of a knife by his face. He is relieved to find he has only fallen asleep and it is his diver's knife, not someone else's. As he gets himself out of bed and rubs his eyes, there is a knock on the door.
'Who is it?'
'It's me' shouts Alex.
Mac opens the door, and Alex climbs into the Winnebago.
'Did you get the GPS,?'
'What do you think?'
Alex hands Mac a small hand held Ground Position Satellite receiver.
'Good man.'
Mac hands Alex his diving valve and tank and picks up a large bag himself, saying, 'Come on, chop chop, we're late.'

'What are we looking for Mac?'
With a big smile on his face, Mac replies 'Gold.'
'Not again.'

At a police station in London, Forbes is on the telephone.
As Mac and Alex drive away from the Winnebago in the Transit van Mac's car phone rings in the Winnebago, unanswered.

Mac and Alex arrive at a house near the beach and get out of the Transit van. They stand in front of the van facing the sea. Mac has a map of the area and the postcard with the Longitude and Latitude readings on it. Alex looks at the co-ordinates on the hand held GPS and then at the ones on the postcard. 'Well it's not out that way Mac.'
'It must be.'
Alex holds the GPS in front of him. 'Here look for yourself.'
Mac takes the GPS from Alex and says, 'It's back there somewhere.'
They get back into the van and drive off. Alex is driving and Mac looking at the GPS readings.
'Keep going Alex. There, turn down that dirt track.'
They turn down the dirt track and eventually reach the end. The ground they are driving on is too rough to continue with the Transit van, so they get out, and start walking. They keep walking and watch the readings on the GPS get closer and closer to the ones written on the postcard. Suddenly Mac shouts 'Bingo.'
They can see a pothole only a few feet from the co-ordinates.

At the pothole, there is a sign with skull and crossbones painted on it and in red letters. Underneath is written 'DANGER UNSAFE AREA'.
Alex looks at Mac. 'Let me guess.'
Mac smiles and then gets on his hands and knees to look down the pothole. He turns back to Alex. 'Have you got a long rope in the van?'
'There's a dive shot line, would that do?'
'That'll do fine.'
Alex returns with the dive line and they secure it to a large rock. Mac ties it around his waist, and Alex hands him a torch saying 'You're absolutely nuts.'
Mac smiles, and replies 'I got a certificate saying I'm not.'
He starts his descent down the pothole.
Alex, concerned, shouts, 'What's down there?'
'Rocks, lots of them.'

Alex waits for a while and sees Mac disappear into the darkness of the pothole. After what seems ages, the rope tightens, and Alex sees Mac begin to climb back out of the pothole. He emerges wet and dirty, but smiling regardless.
He looks at Alex with pleading eyes, 'Fancy pothole diving Alex?'
'NO.' Says Alex in a firm voice.
'Yes you do. It'll be exciting.'
They both go back to the van and start taking the diving equipment to the edge of the pothole. Mac climbs down, and once he gets to the bottom Alex starts to lower the diving equipment down to him.
As he lowers the last piece down he shouts to Mac 'That's it, can't give you any more.'
'Okay Alex, your turn, just watch that support wood as you come down, if you dislodge that I could be buried alive.'
Alex takes a last worried look at the sign that says Danger Unsafe Area, and enters the pothole. The daylight from the pothole entrance is enough to light the hole all the way down to the bottom.

Once Alex reaches the bottom, they quickly start changing into their diving gear. Mac has a dry suit and Alex a wet suit. They help each other with their aqualungs and double-check each other's equipment. Alex ties a line to a rock, so they can find their way back and Mac double checks it's tied ok.
'Course you'll have to watch out for the Mange Eel!'
'Right,' says Alex not wanting to appear stupid. 'What does it look like again?'
Mac smiles. 'It has huge fangs and pink spots and goes straight for the jugular.'
The water is very clear and with the torch, Mac can see it's safe to jump in. Mac jumps first, fins straight down and holding his mask with one hand and the bottom of his tank with the other. He surfaces and turns to face Alex and then gives him the okay sign to jump in.
They check each other's equipment for leaks, and when they are satisfied everything is okay, Mac indicates he will lead and Alex can follow, holding onto the dive line that is attached to the rock.

After a short swim, they see several boxes on the bottom. Mac picks one up and indicates to Alex that they should return to the surface.
They follow the line back and when they are in standing depth, inflate their stab jackets and take their tanks off before going ashore.
Alex remains in the water holding the now floating tanks while Mac climbs out and then takes them from Alex, so he can get out as well.

Once they are both ashore Mac gets his diving knife, and prises open the metal boxes. It is full of yellow squares that look and feel like plasticine. Mac takes one out and smells it.
'What is it?'
'Christmas cake.' jokes Mac. 'Here have a smell.'
Alex takes the block and smells it. 'Marzipan.'
Mac smiles. 'Yes ideal for making exploding Christmas cakes. It's Semtex explosive Alex.'

Suddenly they can hear banging. Alex looks up towards the entrance to the pothole. He can just make out a sledgehammer being used on the support structure to the pothole and shouts, 'Oi, what do you think you're doing?'
Alex jumps back as rocks begin to fall, and then suddenly the whole entrance collapses. Mac and Alex hit the floor, covering their heads with their hands. The noise of the rocks falling is deafening and seems to go on forever. Eventually, it stops.

The place is full of dust, and they can just about breathe, and it is now dark, they feel around for each other.
Mac coughs. 'You all right Alex?'
He feels around to find the torch and then turns it on. It's like shining a headlight in the fog, but he can just see Alex, his face covered in dirt. They use the torch to find the other one and Alex turns that on.
He shines it in Mac's face and asks, 'Has this got something to do with being thrown out the Police Diving Team?'
Mac answers, with an abrupt 'Yes.'
Alex now annoyed says, 'You should have told me.'
'It's become an obsession to find out why, I'm sorry Alex, I didn't mean to put you in danger.'
'Who is it then?'
'I wish I knew.'
There is a short silence as they shine their torches around the pothole.
'This waterway must come in from somewhere and by the looks of things it's our only way out.'
'It probably goes straight down.' replies Alex.
'We can either wait here for Superman or try it.' says Mac, trying to sound reassuring and positive.
Alex, now sounding a little calmer says, 'You know that card I gave you with the shop's telephone number.'
'Yes.'

'Well when we get out of here I want it back.'
Mac gives him a big smile and nods in agreement.

They put their diving gear back on, check their air and find they have an almost full tank each, which, providing they don't go too deep, should last up to an hour.
Alex looks nervous so Mac tries to reassure him again.
'Just relax Alex and don't beat your valve, we'll get out of here I promise you.'
Alex nods. They put their masks on and their diving valves into their mouth and descend to the bottom. They swim for ages in what seems a never-ending tunnel, only lit by the beam of their torch. Mac is leading and Alex follows paying out the line. Mac is suddenly aware Alex is pulling on his fin, he turns around and Alex indicates he has come to the end of the dive line. Mac has to make a decision. He checks his air and realizes they may only have about 30 minutes left. He decides they should swim back. As they swim back the torch gives up the ghost, and they have to feel their way back in complete darkness. Mac is used to this as ninety percent of his diving in the police force was in nil visibility.

Outside the pot-hole the weather is bleak, with dark grey clouds forming. There is a break in the cloud that allows the sun to shine through. At the same time, Mac is looking downwards as they follow the line back and sees a light at the bottom of a deep section of the tunnel. He taps on Alex's tank to attract his attention and indicates by hand motion that they should swim down to the light. As they swim down it gets brighter and brighter, until they end up surfacing in another pothole, but not as deep as the first one. They inflate their stab jackets and swim to a narrow ledge at the side of the pothole.
Mac removes his breathing valve and says to Alex, 'You alright?'
'I won't need the loo for a week.'

They pull their equipment out and there is just room to leave it on the small ledge. They start to climb towards the top of the pothole. As they get to the top, they can see the Transit van is still there and not far away.
'Come on Alex.'
Mac starts to run, followed by Alex.
'What's the hurry?'
'I'll tell you when I know myself.' Mac replies, breathing heavily.
They get into the van, and Mac starts it with the screwdriver.

Mac puts his foot flat on the accelerator and the rear wheels spin, causing a cloud of dust as the van speeds up the track. They head back towards the house near the beach. The van skids to a halt outside the front door of the house. Mac jumps out and runs to the front door. It's locked. He is about to run to the back of the house when a black Mercedes comes crashing through the garage doors.
Mac jumps back out of the car's path and shouts to Alex. 'Stay where you are and keep your seat belt on.'
He jumps back into the Transit van and chases after the Mercedes.
The Mercedes disappears around a corner and out of view. As the Transit takes the corner at speed, the Mercedes is in view again but pulling away fast, the old Transit is far too slow to keep up. Mac realises there is no way he will catch the Mercedes and slows down to a stop. He bangs the dashboard with his fist shouting. 'Damn, damn, damn.'
'Don't blame yourself, there is no way we could catch him in this old heap of shit.'

They return to the house near the beach to see police cars outside and police officers searching the house. Forbes is there.
'Hello Mac, the car was registered in Bruce's name, and he paid cash for the house. Must have been doing a lot of overtime to do that!'
'Who recruited him?'
Forbes shrugs his shoulders. 'Who knows? Someone had access to his record, and picked him as a get rich quick - the dreamer type.'
'Bob was right when he said we were just cannon fodder, Bruce used me as the fall guy.'
Forbes puts his hand on Mac shoulder saying, 'Well he paid the ultimate price, and you can stop taking it personally now and get on with your life.'

Outside a hotel somewhere in the Devon countryside, there is a black Mercedes car parked in the drive. Someone opens the boot to the car. Inside the boot are a suitcase and a sports bag that is slightly open.
The sports bag is crammed full of bank notes. Both suitcase and sports bag are transferred from the Mercedes to the boot of another vehicle. As the boot is closed, Gaynor Evans gets into the car and drives away.

Mac is now in the driving seat of his Winnebago and Forbes is standing by the side window. 'You coming home?'

'The problem is Forbes, I do take it personally, and I will keep in touch.'
Mac starts up his monster motor home and drives away. He can see Forbes in his rear view mirror, and waves his hand out the window, and toots his horn.

THE END (maybe)

A note from the Author Mackenzie Moulton

I am dedicating this book to my friends and colleagues who died whilst serving during my time with the Metropolitan Police Underwater Search Unit. Least we forget them, they are.

Metropolitan Police Underwater Search Unit:
Richard (Dick) Amas and Mark Peers

Essex Police Underwater Search Unit:
Steve Taylor and Andrew Morrison

Some of the names used in this fictitious story relate to some of the real members of the Metropolitan Police Underwater Search Unit I worked with as a police diver.
It in no way relates to the true dedication and professionalism used by them when serving in the Metropolitan police and is written as a compliment to their outstanding work carried out in sometimes difficult and potentially dangerous conditions.

Other names used in the story are also friends and relatives and it in no way relates to their true behaviour and loving characters, but is used as a compliment to their love and friendship towards me.

For the readers who like my story I will also soon be writing true stories about my work with the Metropolitan Police Underwater Search Unit.

Cover Pictures

FRONT COVER

Police Diver Mackenzie Moulton and John (Smoothy) Smith after recovering a Rolls Royce from West India Dock London UK.

REAR COVER

A self-portrait of the Author called 'the standby diver'. It shows the diver sitting in a police boat on the River Thames near Tower Bridge and the old equipment used by the divers back in the 1980's.
The painting is now on permanent display in the Thames Police Association Museum, Wapping High Street, London UK and also in The Public Catalogue Foundation in association with the BBC

Link:
http://www.bbc.co.uk/arts/yourpaintings/artists/mackenzie-william-moulton

My Thanks to John Pilkington for an initial proof reading of the book, and finally and most importantly Janet Chard for a final proof read, and who without my book would not be grammatically correct.

The Author is also an accomplished Artist and musician and examples of his art and music can be found at the website below.

www.mackenziemoultonartist.com

The Police Underwater Search Unit in Victoria Dock London, UK. In the painting are John (Smoothy) Smith, John (Huggy) Hughes, John Newson in the water, Jim Holgate on divers life line and Mackenzie (Mac) Moulton on the helm.

From an Original painting by Mackenzie Moulton

Painting Showing 'The Gun' public house next to the West India Dock entrance. The West India Dock is now known as Canary Wharf

From an original painting by Mackenzie Moulton

Wapping Thames Police Station on the River Thames where the Underwater Search Unit is based.

From an Original Painting by Mackenzie Moulton

And finally here is Mackenzie Moulton the Author recovering a sawn off shotgun that was used in a bank robbery from a canal.

Hope you enjoyed the story.

Mac.

www.ingramcontent.com/pod-product-compliance
Ingram Content Group UK Ltd.
Pitfield, Milton Keynes, MK11 3LW, UK
UKHW041926190726
13854UKWH00003B/1473

9 781446 128206